A Long and Speaking Silence

BOOKS BY NGHI VO

Siren Queen

The Chosen and the Beautiful

Don't Sleep with the Dead

The City in Glass

THE SINGING HILLS CYCLE

The Empress of Salt and Fortune

When the Tiger Came Down the Mountain

Into the Riverlands

Mammoths at the Gates

The Brides of High Hill

A Mouthful of Dust

A Long and Speaking Silence

NGHI VO

TOR PUBLISHING GROUP
NEW YORK

This is a work of fiction. All of the names, characters, organizations, places, and events portrayed in this work are either products of the author's imagination or used fictitiously.

A LONG AND SPEAKING SILENCE

A Tordotcom Book
Published by Tom Doherty Associates / Tor Publishing Group
120 Broadway
New York, NY 10271

www.torpublishinggroup.com

EU Representative: Macmillan Publishers Ireland Ltd, 1st Floor, The Liffey Trust Centre, 117–126 Sheriff Street Upper, Dublin 1, D01 YC43

The Library of Congress Cataloging-in-Publication Data is available upon request.

ISBN 978-1-250-38642-7 (hardcover)
ISBN 978-1-250-38643-4 (ebook)

First Edition: 2026

Printed in the United States of America

10 9 8 7 6 5 4 3 2 1

for everyone trying to get home

A Long and Speaking Silence

Chapter One

"—but back when Old Mo was alive, this place had the best dumpling soup in Feiyu, I'm telling you. This is fine, I'm not saying it's not. It's better than what they're selling down the street for sure, but honestly, it used to be *exceptional.*"

Balancing a tall stack of bowls against their belly, Chih started to turn away, but the woman tugged at their sleeve for emphasis, shaking a finger in their face.

"You be sure to tell the cook that. Less allspice in the dumplings, a shorter simmer. They used to be so tender."

"I certainly will," they lied, pulling their sleeve out of the woman's grasp. "Is there anything else I can get you?"

"Just another bowl of the dumpling soup. Vegetarian this time."

Chih hurried towards the kitchen, almost colliding with the other server who shot them a dirty look and dodged out of their way with the grace of an ox-dancer. Chih would have apologized but then another table, a quartet of prosperous farmers from the highlands by their intricately woven straw cloaks and their tanned faces, waved them over, calling out their orders before Chih had even come to a complete stop.

"Right away, gentlemen!" Chih promised, and two more orders and another four empty bowls set atop their towering stack later, they ducked behind the fluttering curtain into the kitchen.

Certain Compassion's kitchen was hardly less busy than the front of the house, but the rear was left completely open so it was at least cooler. Chih deposited their stack of bowls at the dishwashers' trough before waving down Phiran, the head cook.

"Another vegetarian dumping soup, two plates of Fenghua chicken, one with no cabbage and extra rice, a vegetarian plate, extra spicy, and—and—"

For a moment, they stared at Phiran, a broad wall of a man with shiny twisting burns all up his arms and a cleaver roughly the size of a cavalry saber in his hand, but then a voice from inside their robe piped up.

"One pork-neck soup with extra water lotus root and a half order of fried crackling!"

Chih repeated the order, and Phiran nodded curtly, turning back towards the long spit with his enormous knife. Chih sagged with relief before they remembered they were meant to be preparing the bowls of soup, and they hurried over to the divided cauldron.

"Left is vegetarian, right is pork!" hissed the voice from their robe, and Chih nodded distractedly.

"I know, I know, I'm not that forgetful."

"Really? Then what did the two teenagers from the acting troupe order?"

Almost Brilliant poked her head out from the top of Chih's apron, giving them a sharp look. She was a neixin, a memory spirit in the shape of a young hoopoe. The neixin were the symbol of Chih's home at the Singing Hills abbey, assistants to the researchers and companions to the traveling members of the order. They were not, as Almost Brilliant had been saying for the past three weeks, *waitstaff*.

Chih's mind flashed to the front room, but all that came was a vision of a hungry mob all waving bowls in the air and gesturing with their chopsticks in ways that ranged from impatient to downright threatening.

"I—"

"They haven't yet, because you still haven't gone by to ask! They're seated in the alcove, which is your area!"

It turned out that the teenagers wanted to split an order of fried rice paper between them, the farmers from the highlands were thrilled with the Fenghua chicken, the priest of the empty way wanted a pile of dripping raw greens straight from the cold-water tubs, and mostly people loved the dumpling soup and wanted to tell Chih about it. The restaurant ran like a racing mare in full gallop, only pausing when Chih dropped a pair of plates to thunderous applause and when Phiran came out of the kitchen to shout some ragged-looking women out the door. Otherwise, there was no time to do anything but take orders, make change, run food out to the tables and scraped plates back to the kitchen.

"Come on, cleric, keep up," said the other server as she went by. "You should try this at the end of the pilgrimage season, when all the fancy folks head downriver. Keep hopping!"

Chih didn't feel much like hopping at the moment. Even with Almost Brilliant's memory and the other servers making sure that they didn't mess up too much, they felt like a pig in a chute, too little space to turn around and knives in every direction.

Around sunset, the restaurant finally cleared out, and Phiran shut and latched the front doors. Chih stumbled to the assortment of crates and stools set up in the open area in the kitchen, hanging their apron on the pegs with the rest and collapsing on the bare swept floor. They were so tired they couldn't imagine being hungry. One of the kitchen children, a round-faced girl with a distinct resemblance to a gourd on a stick, approached. She offered them a bowl piled high with chicken over rice and topped with fresh greens, and their hunger woke with a roar.

"Oh *thank* you—"

Before Chih could take the bowl, the restaurant's owner, Sovann, caught sight of it, waving to get her daughter's attention.

"Ah, Little Hulin, not for that one, that's the cleric. Here, give them the vegetarian bowl."

Chih had a moment where they considered actually running off with the chicken. Reluctantly they gave it up in favor of the vegetarian bowl, which to its credit did contain pressed gluten fried in a thick dark sauce. They were still trying to get used to the sharp flavors—the kingdom of Feiyu used some kind of spice that opened their sinuses up and made their nose sting—but it was far better than just the rice and greens that devout clerics were meant to eat.

"I, on the other hand, am no cleric, and I would enjoy some chicken," Almost Brilliant declared, emerging from Chih's robe to perch on a nearby crate. She looked around boldly, affecting lofty indifference as the kitchen children clustered around to offer her scraps of raw chicken from a small earthenware dish. She thanked them graciously before snapping up a strip of clean white skin, and the children watched her do it like it was the most fascinating thing they had ever seen.

"Clever bird," one of the dishwashers commented. "You could sell her to the circus, make some decent money."

Chih had finished their novitiate ten months earlier. Since then, they'd been taking the long slow route to the kingdom of Feiyu from their own home shores in the Anh Empire. This far away, the people who recognized the clerics of Singing Hills or their neixin were growing rarer and rarer, and Chih still wasn't quite sure how to handle comments like this one, which was like suggesting someone sell their sibling.

"I could never," they said honestly. "She's as much a part of the abbey as I am."

"And I should like to see you try," Almost Brilliant said, tossing down another scrap of chicken. "Imagine, *me* working in a circus."

"There are storytellers in the circus," said Little Hulin shyly. "You tell stories, don't you, honored one?"

"No one calls *me* honored one," Chih muttered into their bowl, but Almost Brilliant preened.

"I listen to stories, and I remember them perfectly. I will never forget what I have heard, and I carry with me the memories of generations of my kind. But perhaps I can be persuaded to tell a story or two, if I'm told some in return."

Chih sat back with their food, wryly amused and only a touch resentful at how easy it was for a talking bird to do the job Chih was supposed to be doing. When they asked, no one seemed to have time for them, or they thought Chih was selling something, or they wanted to sell something to Chih.

They listened with half an ear as Almost Brilliant told the story about the old woman who prepared the feast for the end of the world. Every time she looked around, her grandchildren came to pick skin off the roast meat and dumplings from the soup and even whole chickens off the table so that she would never be ready for the great ladies of fire, flood, blood, and misery to come dine at her house. It was the version they told in western Anh, where Chih and Almost Brilliant were both born, with the chicken smashed flat under a weight before being cooked whole and fluffy rice flour buns dipped in the soup.

In return, Little Meng, Sovann's nephew, offered up the story of how he had seen a cat walking along the river last year, who was so white that she glowed in the dark. He'd called a dozen names after her, Pearl, Little Treasure, Eye in the Night, because in Feiyu, if you could guess a cat's name, she would come home with you and live with you all her life.

"Did you guess right?" Almost Brilliant asked with interest.

"No. She turned around, and she called my name," Little Meng said. "She took it, and now I have to be Little Meng instead of—"

"That's enough. No reason to talk about that," said Sovann firmly.

"Wait, what happens if a cat calls your name?" Chih blurted out, and they shrank back from Sovann's glare. "I. Um. Sorry."

"Thank you for telling me what happened to you," Almost Brilliant said loudly. "Now I shall tell you about the Crimson Princess who fell in love with the rider in the storm and what became of her."

Chih ducked their face down to hide their red cheeks.

They wished there was a way to call errant words back into their mouth so they could swallow them. The older clerics made it look so easy when Chih traveled with them, navigating cities and customs with consummate ease. Now it felt as if Chih couldn't go more than three days without doing something that made everyone around them angry and wary of the stranger who wanted to hear their stories.

The clerics of Singing Hills are meant to mark down the stories of the world, to hear and to remember and to witness, they thought morosely. *Maybe I* should *be waiting tables.*

They winced. They had broken four plates total today, which was less than they had broken yesterday at least, but their career in food service looked no more promising than their career as a cleric of Singing Hills.

Chih's thoughts were interrupted by the approach of a pair of young men. They were neatly dressed, but unlike the restaurant staff, who wore robes and trousers similar to what Chih was familiar with in Anh, the young men wore long tunics over wide trousers that gathered at the ankle. The women Phiran had thrown out earlier were dressed in similar clothing, they remembered, albeit more shabbily.

Now Phiran rose from his stool, squaring up to the men with unusual severity.

"There's a Thousand Hands temple if you go up the street and take a left after the fish market. They'll have food for you if they're not out by now. It's better to go early."

Chih's chest tightened at Phiran's words, their own food sitting colder in their belly. They started to say something, a cleric *should* say something, but one of the young men was already shaking his head.

"No, thank you. We are not looking for food. We are looking for work. Surely with the festival going on, you need workers?"

"No, we don't. Try at the barbecue place down the way."

"We'll work hard," the second young man burst out. "Anything, it doesn't matter, big or small, we can do it."

The cook smiled thinly, no humor in it and a bare skim of courtesy over his disbelief.

"I'm sure the barbecue place will appreciate it," he said pointedly.

Chih could see the moment they both gave up, shoulders dropping before rising again, hunched as if in preparation for a blow. Phiran followed them out, pausing in the door to watch them walk away down the road. He shook his head before returning to his stool, and Chih realized that they must have had a less than neutral look on their face because he turned his scowl on them.

"I don't need to hear it, cleric. I don't have any work for them. Anyway, they're the ones who snatched your purse and got you stuck waiting tables."

They had found their purse missing as they'd gotten off the ferry, the strings clipped neatly and left dangling from their sash. By the time they noticed, the people who had shared the ferry with them, mostly refugees from the Verdant Islands, had disembarked, and there was no chance of recovering their money. It probably *was* a refugee who'd cut their purse strings, but as Cleric Thien used to say, anyone who thought that a traveling cleric had money worth stealing almost certainly needed it more than the cleric did. Still, a thorn stung Chih's tongue and would keep stinging it unless they spoke.

"Those men?" they asked in surprise. "I do not think I have ever seen them before. They were not on the ferry with me when I arrived, and I do not believe I met them in the street. Do you recognize them perhaps? Have they stolen from someone else here to make you think that?"

It was, as things went, the gentlest of reprimands, but Phiran's scowl deepened.

"You're a foreigner yourself, you wouldn't understand," he began, sounding a bit like a kettle about to boil, but then Almost Brilliant shouted, "And *CRACK* went the lightning!" so loudly that everyone turned to look at her.

"And the Crimson Princess fell down, down, down, through the forest of the gales and the cloud gardens and the meadows of the soft breezes, until she crashed headlong into the Cauldron Sea. She struck the water so hard that half of the green whales that lived there were splashed all the way to the Mother Sea on the far side of the world. That is why green whales sing the same songs no matter where you find them, because they are trying to find their brothers and their wives and their fathers and their friends that were lost when the Crimson Princess fell."

"What happened to her?" asked Little Hulin, the kind of listener every storyteller hopes for, and Almost Brilliant trilled with satisfaction.

"She received such a shock when she struck the water that her thoughts scattered and turned into a thousand silver fish. It took a very long time before she was able to catch them, and she would never have managed it at all without the help of the warrior monk Boi Ca, who was a bird before he prayed and fasted and became a man. But that is another story, and this one is done."

The kitchen children of course clamored to hear the story of Boi Ca and the Crimson Princess, and Almost Brilliant fluffed out her wings modestly.

"I should love to tell it, but I think it's someone else's turn to tell a story. Little Hulin, perhaps, do you have a story for us?"

"I don't know any stories," Little Hulin began fretfully, but Chih spoke up, grateful that Sovann had turned away from the foolishness of birds and archivists.

"Everyone knows stories," they said, grateful at least to be on safer ground. "A story can be long or short, happy or sad. All a story needs to do is to tell us something you know that you would like us to know."

"Um. I could tell you about the girl who ran off to play at the ghost palace? If you wanted?"

There were perhaps hundreds of variations on the story

of Sweet Nhu, who ran off to the ghost palace that docked next to her house one night. Sometimes she was a nun or a brothel girl or a princess or a pig farmer, and sometimes she wanted to dance or to follow a clever man or a veiled woman or to hear a song that drifted down to her while she slept, but the story was the same. She danced or she kissed someone or she heard her song, and when she returned, the world had leaped forward a hundred years and everyone she left behind was dead except for her littlest brother, who was an old, old man.

"I would love to hear your story," Chih said, setting their empty bowl aside and pulling out their recording materials. Chih was suddenly grateful that the person who had taken their purse hadn't taken their notebooks as well, coarse sheets of paper bound with tough hemp thread. They weren't amazing at waiting tables, but they could do it. They didn't know if they could sit still and let a story go by.

"Well, there was a girl named Amo, and she. She lived in a house with her mother and her father and her baby brother behind a big lim tree just-like-the-one-in-front-of-our-house. She was a very good girl except that she always wanted to hear stories, and she would bother everyone until they stopped their work and told them to her."

That was a new one to Chih, and apparently to Almost Brilliant as well, who cocked her head back and forth before going stiller than a real bird would.

Little Hulin told the story with stops and starts, pausing sometimes to ask her mother for the right details. Sovann, as stout and solid as her husband the cook, offered up the corrections with amusement, and Chih noted down the places where Little Hulin stopped and her mother began.

Even with the addition of a girl with eyes painted over her eyes who helped the heroine climb out of the bedroom of the sleepless king and an interlude with a blind spider woman that Chih thought could be used to nest more stories inside the one being told, it was still and all the tale of Sweet Nhu. She was Amo in the Feiyu, Joolee in the northern confederation, and a hundred other names in a hundred other places. Even as diligent as they were, Chih felt themself nodding along at the expected beats in the story, writing fast to catch up when Little Hulin triumphantly got to the end.

"And her brother was there, and he was old, old, old and wrinkled. He was mad at her because she had been gone so long. Amo cried and cried, and finally, she went far, far away, and all she took with her was the robe of the sleepless king and the drum of the crane woman and the story she was told."

Something about the way that Little Hulin said the last words made Chih look up. They realized they were tilting their head in imitation of Almost Brilliant and straightened.

"Is that the end of the story?"

Something about Chih's voice must have betrayed their eagerness, because Little Hulin went red, covering her face with one splayed hand.

"Little Hulin? Are you sure that's the end of the story?" they asked, and the small girl drew back fretfully, looking up at her mother.

"That's all of it, cleric," said Sovann. She was still friendly, friendlier than her husband at any rate, but there was a warning note to her voice, and Chih couldn't even blame her. It was bad practice to drag stories out of anyone, let alone someone who had only been talking for a few years.

"Thank you very much for your story, Little Hulin of Luntien. I have written it down here, and when I return to my home in western Anh, it will be entered into the archives where people may enjoy it for years and years to come."

Impulsively, Chih bowed over their knees, their hands clasped in front of them. There were snorts of laughter from the adults to see a cleric, no matter how down on their luck, bow to a little girl, but Little Hulin gasped in delight, scrambling to her feet and crossing her hands over her heart as they did in Feiyu and bowing low twice to repay the honor.

"That's enough," Sovann said firmly, touching Hulin's back. "Time's past for you and Little Meng to say goodnight to the family and take your baths."

Obediently, the children bid goodnight to their elders

and followed Sovann off, but then to Chih's surprise, Little Hulin turned and ran back to them.

"I forgot!" she exclaimed. "Amo cried and cried and *cried,* but then the Queen of Birds took pity on her and carried her over the desert and over the sea and past the stars all the way to where the hills sing songs, and she and her story lived there for always."

She bowed deeply again and ran after her mother, and Chih's mind buzzed like a hive full of bees.

Chapter Two

Sixteen years ago, there was terrible flooding in the empire of Anh. The Hu River and its fourteen children, some as great as the Ohono River, some as gentle and beautiful as the Thu, forgot the bargain they had made with the people of the west and rose up out of their banks. They flooded the crops and drowned the animals. They came to sit in the parlors and sleep in the bedrooms of the people of the west, and when they were done, they lifted the houses up and carried them away as if they were guest gifts.

Chih's parents, so they'd been told, had come all the way from the banks of the Boneyard, a mean and narrow river that nonetheless ran deep enough to wipe out most of their clan—where their village had been, there were only treetops reaching mournfully out of the water. Their parents had already come a long way, and had a long way to go yet to reach distant relatives in Zhou. They had five children, and they decided their chances, all of their chances, would be better if they left their youngest, who was only two, with some traveling clerics they met along the way.

Chih knew that memories didn't properly start until children were around three or four. If they remembered something from the age of two, it was likely that they had been told a thing so many times they thought they remembered, or perhaps they only dreamed they remembered. Still, Chih remembered being carried piggyback between Cleric Sun and Cleric Thien as they passed through the woods and came to the broad meadows. They remembered seeing a rise of craggy stone too short to be called a mountain, and backed up against it, low and gray and humble, an ancient stone fortress.

"Here we are," Cleric Thien said. "We're home."

As they spoke, the wind started to blow, and over the grass came a high and hollow sound that pierced them straight through the chest. It was an eerie sound, and they shivered and buried their face in Cleric Sun's shoulder with a sob. They had never heard anything like it before. They missed their parents and their siblings.

Cleric Thien's neixin, Myriad Virtues, neat and proper in every way, fluttered to Chih's shoulder. They could remember how heavy she had seemed to them then, how large, when she was actually among the smaller neixin of the aviary.

"You mustn't cry, Baby Chih," she said. "Listen. It is the song of Singing Hills. It is welcoming you home."

And it was, and it had, and now Cleric Thien and Myriad Virtues were investigating a haunting close to the capital, and Cleric Sun had finally gotten sick of everyone and started their own archive by the sea, and Chih was a cleric themself, and Little Hulin's story echoed in their dreams.

During the festival, the restaurant didn't open until it was time for late breakfast. Everyone was still sleeping when Chih woke up and slipped out of the kitchen into the lowering gray day. It was already hot with a heavy dampness that would make everything harder to bear, the kind of heat that turned everyone, man and animal alike, restless and snappish. Chih washed with a pail from the rain barrel, and when they were clean, they whistled into the yard.

"There you are," said Almost Brilliant. "I have been waiting for ages."

"Oh? And were there no insects to keep you company?"

She fluttered from the edge of the low roof to settle on Chih's shoulder. They had been partnered for less than a year, but it was astonishing how quickly her weight and her presence had become familiar, even if she could be a rather pompous know-it-all sometimes.

"Yes, there were plenty, especially after I shooed off the brown birds that usually live in the lim tree. I have had a fine breakfast, and now I am ready to work."

"Breakfast isn't on for a while yet—"

"Then you'll have plenty of time to go meet with the harbormasters. Or did you have some other ideas about what a cleric ought to be doing first thing in the morning?"

Somewhat begrudgingly, Chih pulled on their sandals and their indigo robe. Without the apron and with their shaved head, at least they looked like a cleric now, though most clerics didn't smell so persistently of fried food.

"Actually, I was thinking about Little Hulin's story last night," Chih said as they made their way down to the river. "She mentioned a hill that sings songs and how Amo's story had a place to live forever. That sounds a great deal like home, doesn't it?"

Almost Brilliant's head swiveled left and right, her feathered crest tickling Chih's cheek as she did so.

"It sounds like the story of Sweet Nhu and a hundred others, told to us by a child who was half falling asleep. It sounds like a coincidence to me. A charming one, but without further corroboration, nothing but a coincidence."

"It was just a thought," Chih grumbled, and Almost Brilliant hooted with irritation.

"Think about the things you want to ask the harbormasters. Do you have the questions you were given?"

Chih did, in a waxed envelope that Cleric Duc had passed to them before they set sail from Anh. Cleric Duc was thorough to a fault and had included a brief write-up of the city itself as well as Chih's objectives there.

Luntien stretched out east and west from the banks of the Ya-lé River, the largest city until one reached the capital to the north, and it was known as the General of the Water. By the time the Ya-lé River reached the sea to the south, it was a tame thing, a roaring girl whittled down to a proper lady. In Luntien, however, the river remembered what it truly was, and its soft thunder rolled behind every word spoken on its banks.

At the end of the day, Luntien was a river city, full of motion, people and stories coming in and out, and nowhere was this more evident than at the docks. Even at this early hour, it was busy, and at Chih's tentative questions, a canal worker impatiently pointed out a harbormaster, a man in a green sash fanning himself with a braided straw fan and already irritated with the day. Chih started towards him, but then the brazen bell on the far end of the docks rang, another ferry pulling in.

"Oh for the—another one already!"

He strode down the dock to meet the ferry, and Chih blinked at the ragged figures aboard. More Verdant Island refugees, they realized, and the ferry bobbed in the water as the harbormaster argued with the ferryman, gesturing emphatically upriver. Chih found themself staring at the people on the ferry, twenty or so, with just under half of them children.

"Where could he be trying to send them?" Chih found themself asking in a hushed voice, as if it were something secret to whisper about.

"Upriver, by the look of it," said Almost Brilliant. Her

words were cool, but there was a waver to them Chih hadn't heard before.

"Luntien is what, the tenth town up the river from the sea? They've come such a long way already."

The clerics of Singing Hills could lay the dead to rest, stand as witness for contracts of many kinds, and bless a baby or an endeavor, but they were mostly concerned with their archives and the gathering of knowledge. They were not martial arts masters like clerics of Bangala, or famed doctors like the clerics devoted to the Twins of Jun-li. Even if the clerics of Singing Hills were recognized as one of the most singular orders of Anh, Chih had no authority here, but they couldn't take their eyes off the children on the ferry, the ones who leaned against their parents' hips, the ones who swayed on their feet and whose faces had clean streaks through the dirt where the tears had dried.

"All right, that's enough," Chih muttered, and they hurried down the dock. "Ah, excuse me!"

The ferryman and the harbormaster turned towards Chih, both of them visibly restraining their impatience when they saw the indigo robe and the shaved head. Chih came to a complete stop before they started speaking, remembering to smile as they did so.

"Good morning! I'm Chih! That is, I'm *Cleric* Chih from the Singing Hills abbey in Anh."

"Yes, here for the yearly water table readings," said

the harbormaster. "A moment, cleric. If you go to the command office back the way you came, you can get a cup of tea and something to eat while you wait. I'll be finished here and with you in—"

"As. As a matter of fact. I'm not here for the survey right now," Chih said with desperate brightness. "I'm here about these people."

"You are?" the ferryman asked skeptically, and Chih nodded.

"I am. I *am.* You see. The temple in town, the one for the Lady of the Thousand Hands, they're taking in refugees, and it would be a shame to—"

That was apparently enough for the people on the ferry. They surged forward, not waiting for the ferry to be properly docked before they jumped the small gap to the planks. The harbormaster turned with an offended cry, but the ferryman shrugged, and now people were handing their children over the gap while two large men stood by to keep the harbormaster from interfering. One of them waved to Chih.

"Cleric, where's that temple?"

For a moment, Chih's mind was nothing but the sound of wind echoing over a bleak grassland. They weren't *cleric,* they were *novice,* specifically Novice Chih, assisting Cleric Thien or Cleric Yu-ching. Then they remembered no, they were Cleric Chih now, and they should have made a note of the directions to the temple of the Lady of the Thousand Hands.

"Um, it's up the street, you get to the gates to the docks, and I think you turn left—"

The harbormaster sputtered, exclaimed something that Chih didn't catch but one of the refugee women uttered an angry cry. She gave him a hard shove, he gave her one in return, and the shout went up. The ferryman was cursing everyone who had turned a simple fare into a brawl, some of the refugees ran away down the dock, some rivermen from the other slips ran forward to see the commotion, and in trying to calm things down, Chih got pushed straight into the water.

There was actually a moment, between their feet leaving the planks and hitting the green water below, where everything was as sharp-edged and bright as broken crystal. They saw Almost Brilliant throwing herself clear, her wings spread and dark against the morning sky. They saw the faces of the refugees, how angry they were and how frightened, and they saw the rivermen coming forward to lend aid, though it was not clear who they might be helping or how.

Then there was the shock of water, still chilled from the night, and Chih landed exactly wrong. Their mouth, still open from a yelp, filled immediately with the river. They splashed to stay afloat, coughing wildly to get the water out of their lungs. By the time they could conceivably call for help, the commotion had moved on, the refugees forcing their way to land, the rivermen calling for others to come.

Oh, that's going to be a mess, they thought in dismay.

There was no easy way back up onto the deck. The dry season had dropped the water level, and Chih had to paddle all the way to where the planking stopped and the muddy bank began. They wrung out their robe as best they could before putting it on again, and as they were inspecting their bundle of papers to find out what could be saved, there was a warning hoot followed by the weight of Almost Brilliant landing on their shoulder.

"Don't scold me," they said, wishing they sounded firmer. "They just looked so tired and—"

"Nothing ate my heart while you weren't looking," Almost Brilliant snapped. "You were right to step in, though you might have done so more smoothly and with the dignity inherent to your office."

She paused, her head darting left and right as she considered.

"But still, it was good that you did. The places farther upriver get increasingly smaller and poorer. Luntien has courier services and regular deliveries back down the river and north to Beixia, so it will be easier for them to make contact with their families and friends."

"How do you know all that?"

Almost Brilliant puffed herself up, briefly looking quite round as she did so.

"Because I listen," she said sternly. "*And* I read Cleric Duc's briefing documents."

"I read them too! You just have a better memory than I do."

"I have a better memory than everyone. Anyway, dry off more quickly than that. You need to get a move on."

"Why?"

"Because you didn't mind your purse, and now you have to wait tables."

Chih glanced up at the sun, now higher in the sky than they had thought it would be, and jogged towards the road. They were at least somewhat drier by the time they got back to the restaurant, though they were too late for food. They served until past noon on a rumbling stomach, and then they were allowed to sit in the back with a plate of fried patties the size of large hen eggs. The patties were mashed root vegetables mixed with rice, dunked in batter, and then dropped into terrifyingly hot oil. Three of them were enough for a decent meal, and Chih gratefully ate four, huffing cool air into their mouth when they found how fresh they were. The last one had finely minced pork mixed in with the filling, and Chih ate it with no small amount of private glee. Perhaps the best thing about being on their own on the road was that there were no senior clerics around to insist on best vegetarian practices.

Chih was surreptitiously swiping the fried crumbs from their plate with their finger and licking them up when a young boy came to the rear of the kitchen. Dressed in the clothing of the Verdant Islands, he hovered outside nervously before Phiran went to ask him his business, and then he disappeared quickly, as if aware he was not welcome. Chih blinked when Phiran called over to them.

"Cleric, you're wanted at the temple of the Lady of the Thousand Hands."

"Er? Why?"

Phiran scowled reflexively, but Chih was too tired or perhaps too newly fed to shrink back.

"Do I look like I take messages for you? Some Verdant Island people want you. Go. Don't go. It makes no matter to me as long as you finish your shift."

It was likely too much to expect to get time off of work to do their actual work, and Chih couldn't really afford to miss a shift until their stipend caught up with them in a few weeks. Reluctantly, they put their apron back on and braced for the rush. The crowd was, if anything, even thicker than it had been the night before, more travelers in town to vend at the festival, to worship at the temples for luck and safety when the rains came, or simply to meet up with friends and family.

Everyone was cheerful, happy to yell their orders again when Chih had to ask them to repeat themselves, but an ugly undercurrent emerged when a pair of Verdant Island men appeared. There was some confusion, whether they wanted to work for food or whether they wanted food for free—Phiran and Sovann both emerged from the kitchen, raising their voices to see the men back into the streets. It should have been the end of it, but the animosity lingered both in the front of the house and in the kitchen.

"Lazy," proclaimed a traveling apothecary with his backframe of bottles leaned against his legs. "They'll never work a day in their lives if they can help it."

"They're not," replied a scholar with an earnest Anh accent. "It is only that the Verdant Islands have no education, no system of scholars, no university. One might say that they simply do not know better."

"One *might*—"

In the kitchen, Sovann attacked a side of pork, reducing it to a pile of tidy ribs for marinade and meat for the sausage maker.

"I don't care what they do," she muttered as Chih passed by. "I truly don't. They just can't do it here."

Then where? Chih wanted to ask, because if Sovann had any ideas, they certainly wanted to hear them, but then they were handed a tray loaded down with six bowls overfilled with soup and sent back to the dining room.

By the time they brought in the last stack of plates, they were definitely shaky on their feet and they weren't sure they'd ever stop smelling like cooking oil and soy sauce. They started for the nearest stool, but then Phiran seized their arm. For a moment, Chih froze, every lesson of how to fend off muggers falling straight out of their head, but then Phiran lifted their hand in his as if declaring a winner at a village wrestling match.

"And for the cleric, one hundred years of good fortune and the golden duck, because they have made it through an entire damned shift without breaking *one! Single! Dish!*"

Chih choked on an astonished laugh as the kitchen broke out in applause, faces that had been nothing but closed and irritated with them opening like gates. They stared around in surprise, and Phiran clapped them on the back.

"Go on, let Soshi make you up a plate. Have some of the wine, too, if you want. You've been working hard, and—why under the great blue sky are you *crying*?"

Chih tried to explain it, and then just started laughing, shaking their head.

"It's stupid, it's stupid," they said as the server who kept hipping them out of her way patted their arm, and the dishwasher whose face they had never seen gave them a hug. "I'm sorry, it's just. I've never been this *bad* at something before!"

"You think you're bad?" Sovann hooted, slapping her thighs. "Bich spilled soup over two tables at once!"

The server, Bich, waved both her hands at Sovann, shaking her head.

"No, no, no," she scolded like a jay. "I spilled soup over *three* tables and knocked over the fourth table's drinks. Tell it right, boss!"

They pushed Chih down onto one of the stools, and this time, Chih got noodles drowned in a pork-neck broth, smothered with carrots and wilted sawtooth herbs, spicy and so delicious they almost started crying again.

"That's from the west like you are," Sovann explained. "My ma brought it over, said it was a good-time meal. We got it for festivals and weddings. When my brother moved to Beixia to run overland shipping for a big company, she made so much we invited the whole street in. You can pick around the pork if you need to, she said clerics in the west could do that and still be within their vows."

"I will not be doing that," Chih said, already picking out one of the neck bones to gnaw off the fatty gristle.

The food was good, but what was better was the way the kitchen changed, Bich and the other server Soshi shouting out their worst serving mishaps while Phiran told them how they'd tormented apprentices back in his day.

"You get some chili seeds in the pan, see, and you cook them dry and scrape them out so the poor kid's none the wiser. Then you hand it over, still hot, and you tell him to get it clean immediately, no waiting. Water hits that pan, and the steam that comes up will make their eyes swell straight shut!"

The staff laughed as if it was the funniest thing they'd ever heard, and Chih did as well while having the sneaking suspicion that that was a deeply unkind thing to do to someone who just wanted to learn to cook. But the food was good, and even if Almost Brilliant grumbled disapprovingly, she still ate her chicken.

It was getting on to dark by the time Chih was able to refuse the last cracker and another sip of wine ("Honestly, what kind of cleric *are* you?") and slip out the back. Before they could make their way down the road to the temple, however, Bich whistled them down, handing them a bag of crackers that was about the size of a four-year-old and a smaller bag of somewhat squashy citrus fruits. At Chih's startled look, Bich snorted.

"You're going to the temple, right?" When Chih blinked, she rolled her eyes in a way that was deeply familiar from the first day, when Chih couldn't figure out which chili sauce was hot, which one was sweet, and which one was smoky. "You know, the temple of the Lady of the Thousand Hands? Where the Verdant Islanders are?"

"Er, yes?"

She pointed at the bags Chih held.

"The citrus fruits are leftovers from when Sovann made sauce. The crackers will be soggy by morning, so we'll be doing another big batch then anyway. Get them out of here."

She crossed her arms over her chest, daring Chih to say anything about it. Chih considered.

Bich dressed like Sovann and the other women did, and she spoke like them as well, but she wore hollow bone spools in her earlobes, big enough to stick a finger through. Her mother had come to the kitchen a few days ago for a quick meal, and she'd had the same spools.

Sometimes the customers asked Chih about those spools, and some were nicer about it than others.

"Where are you from?" It was out before Chih could stop it, their curiosity slipping by their sense, and Bich gave them a flat look.

"I live with my ma and my sister and her kid two streets over," she said. She was ready to fight if Chih wanted to argue the point—*no, where are you* really *from*—but Chih was too relieved at being offered a second chance.

"I don't know much about Luntien," they said finally. "I was wondering, perhaps, if I could sit down with you, and you could tell me about it."

She batted her eyelashes at Chih, pressing two fingertips against her plump cheeks as if widening her smile.

"Wait, are you asking me to go walking with you by the water? I'll have to borrow the snake shawl from my sister! I'll have to get some paint for my lips!"

Chih's cheeks went flaming red, and they nearly dropped the bags of food. Bich laughed and gave them a friendly smack on their shoulder. At least, they assumed it was friendly. It was exactly the same as the smack they got when they needed to get out of her way.

"Calm down, cleric. Sure. We can talk about Luntien if you want. Right now, I'm going to watch a puppet show with my girlfriends, and you're off to do something boring and virtuous."

She shrugged as if none of it mattered to her, but as

they turned, Chih caught her making a quick gesture with her hand, something complicated with her fingers down by her side.

"What's that—ow!"

Almost Brilliant fluttered to Chih's other shoulder, allowing Chih to rub the earlobe she'd tugged.

"You were doing so well," Almost Brilliant said primly. "I should hate for you to fall on your face now."

Chih started to snap that they were fine, and then they sighed, nodding. The clerics who had taught them always counseled patience, but it was a hard lesson to learn when the whole world felt like a storehouse of strange and wonderful things, none of which anyone had bothered to record or report.

Chapter Three

The darkness thickened, and as Chih walked along the main thoroughfare, lanterns went up, red like luck, yellow like joy, green like love, every color except white for mourning. The restaurants had closed their doors, but the taverns were just opening them, setting out signs with their menus, sending out children to tug on the sleeves of passersby, promising drinks from as far away as the city of Anh and the best whole fried sparrows in Feiyu. Chih was still trying to find a good time to try sparrow. It wasn't much eaten where they came from, and they didn't serve it at all at Certain Compassion. The curled claws under the golden batter gave them an instinctive horrified lurch, but they were determined to try it before they left.

The night vendors had come out with racks of festival charms mounted to their backs and portable grills set up on the street. During the day, the road was occupied mainly by pedestrians and ox carts, but any ox drovers who tried to come through now would find the way completely impassable, blocked as it was with acrobats, singers, impromptu theater troupes, and the large box stages of the puppeteers that Bich had been so eager to see.

Some dancers lifted an enormous segmented dragon puppet over their heads on poles, marching in step as their dragon snaked through the crowd. It was astonishing how easy it was to only see the painted tin puppet. The dancers themselves didn't wear anything special, instead choosing to blend in with the celebrants. Chih couldn't help staring after the dancing dragon, how its head wove left and right to the beat of the nearby drum, how the tail swung to the same rhythm as if it really was one creature. It wasn't a real dragon, they knew that, but Chih couldn't escape their conviction that it was still real, real and made of tin, perhaps, but real nevertheless.

"It's like another city," Chih said, turning around wide-eyed to see a man in a tiger mask go by. When he caught them looking, he flexed to show off arms bigger than Chih's thighs before handing them a leaflet for a tumbling troupe where all the tumblers were animals that had been transformed into humans.

"Perhaps," replied Almost Brilliant, snipping her beak at a too-curious drunk. "But one imagines the way to the temple is always the same."

"Straight and true as virtue itself," Chih sighed.

They reluctantly passed the leaflet to someone else and

held up a hand to shelter Almost Brilliant as they ducked and wove their way up the street.

They had grown up accompanying their elders, seen temples that were little more than a grove of beribboned trees and temples that could have been palaces themselves. Temples were as different as those who tended them, but temples to the Lady of the Thousand Hands, no matter how humble they were or how grand, were never permitted to bar their doors.

The cult of the Lady of the Thousand Hands had been established in Feiyu for a long time. Her temple was one of the biggest in Luntien, a large building with an elegantly tiled conical roof surrounded by a scattering of smaller buildings and a wide open space circled by a gateless stone wall. In better times, that open space was used for religious convocations and conferences or perhaps for weddings. Right now, it was being put to grimmer use.

Even from the road, Chih could smell the high reek of too many people in one place, the smell like a wall itself, and they gagged before they remembered to breathe evenly and calmly. Chih passed through the gap in the stone wall without challenge and found themself in a campground, tents set up in crooked rows and made from a wide assortment of tarps and blankets.

If Luntien was one city at night and another one during the day, Chih found a third city in the shelter of the temple. From where they stood, they could see a dozen small fires with people gathered around them cooking their dinner in brass pots or on makeshift grills. When one person finished, they took their food and returned to their tent so that another could take their place. The people who ate looked as if even that motion exhausted them, and when someone briefly raised their voice in a song, it was shouted down impatiently.

"Yes?"

Chih jumped, blinking at the older man who stood before them, his hands clasped at his back. By his clothing, he was from the Verdant Islands, and he stood with his feet planted as if he had grown there, in the exact spot between Chih's gaze and his people.

"I'm Cleric Chih of the Singing Hills. Um, I was told I was asked for?" They corrected themself. "I was asked for, though I'm sorry to say I was not told who did the asking."

On their shoulder, Almost Brilliant shifted her weight from foot to foot.

"And I am Almost Brilliant, neixin of Singing Hills, of the line of Ever Victorious and Always Kind. What I hear will never be forgotten."

The man's face cleared, and suddenly he seemed less imposing than he had a moment before: one moment an immovable wall that wanted to know why it should not fall on you, and the next simply a man with carefully mended sleeves and his hands held open.

"You were the ones at the docks this morning," he said. "You were the ones who told my cousin about this place. You got the harbormaster to let them off the ferry."

"Not really," Chih had to say truthfully. "I told them about the temple, but I think I was at best a momentary distraction."

"You looked like a monkey when you went into the water!" called a teenager, and she uttered a short primate shriek that cut off abruptly as she threw her hands in the air like water splashing upwards. This won a ripple of laughter from the people around them, and Chih had to grin ruefully as well, because it was probably a pretty funny image.

"Ha Beili, shut your mouth," snapped someone nearby. "No one wants to hear the stupidity that falls out of it."

"It's fine—" Chih started, but the man shook his head.

"Forgive us, honored cleric," he said, certainly far too humbly to be speaking to Chih. "We have asked you here, and we are humiliating ourselves."

He bowed low, and Chih's first impulse was to drag him back up with shock. He was old enough to be their father or perhaps even their grandfather, and it wasn't right that he should bow—

"No," Almost Brilliant hissed in their ear. "Do not make this *worse.*"

They had asked for a cleric, and Chih realized that they didn't want these people to have asked for one more thing they couldn't have. For a moment, they had no idea what to do, and then they remembered.

They straightened, smiling and nodding when the man stood.

"It's no matter. It was a rather undignified position to find myself in as well, and we shall speak no more about it."

"Thank you for your grace, cleric, and your patience as well with young fools."

The teenager, Ha Beili, shrank back. It struck Chih that at most, they were only a year or two older than she was, and they beckoned her closer. She came with a worried look, skirting warily around the man who glared at her, blinking when Chih handed her the bags that Bich had given to them.

"You look like you know everyone. Please offer these around. They're from the restaurant where I'm staying at the moment."

The teenager ran off with the food, and Chih turned back to the elder, more confident.

"Now how can I help you?"

As it turned out, Vang Kao and his family were fishermen, like most of the families camped within the temple walls. He was no headman, no clan leader at all.

"They left first," he explained, careful to keep any trace of bitterness out of his voice. "They were the ones who knew the ships' captains and when they would come to shore. Their households were gone by the time the trouble started. We grabbed what we could when the fighting came, took our own boats out to the shipping lanes, and hoped for the best."

Chih had heard of the conflict, of course: Ue County

and Anh's historical feud over the colonies of the south seas sprung up again for the first time in a generation. With the Empress of Salt and Fortune so ill, the south was seizing its chance.

"When I was a boy, a cleric from the Singing Hills came to Muyi with a bird like the one on your shoulder. What was told to them was remembered, and carried wherever the cleric walked, and the cleric walked far."

"This is true. We are historians, primarily. We record what we see and hear, and it is entered into the archives of Singing Hills in the west."

"We do not need historians. Begging your pardon, cleric, but we are not yet ready to be history. No, what we need is to find our families, the ones we lost. Where are you going after this?"

"Well, after the festival, I'm heading north, towards Beixia, the capital." Chih hesitated. "There is a temple to the Lady of the Thousand Hands there, a large one, I believe, but no guarantee that any of your family have ended up there."

"As you might guess, honored cleric, I have learned that there is very little in the world that is guaranteed. We need names sent. We want them to know who lived, who left. And who didn't."

In the end, it was easiest for Chih and Almost Brilliant to move from tent to tent, talking to the head of each household. Most of the time, it was a man who was around the same age as Vang Kao. Sometimes it was a young boy with a haunted look in his eyes, prompted by his mother or oldest sister to list the clan connections that spidered out from the mother's line, inheritance and kinship passed primarily through nephews rather than through sons. Chih filled page after page with names and cramped family trees, Almost Brilliant correcting them where they misplaced a line to a cousin or an uncle. It was troubling to think of how much information could be lost with a dropped or misheard character. It was horrifying how easy it was to do so.

For all the weight of fear and hope and pain, this work was deadly dull, and more than once, Chih had to walk beyond the walls to clear their head and shake out their hand.

"Have the clerics of the temple here been keeping track of the people who pass through?" Chih asked at one point, and the very young man they were talking to, sitting cross-legged with one fist planted on his knee in uncomfortable imitation of his elders, shook his head derisively.

"Why should they when they want us gone as soon as possible?"

"The temple of the Lady of the Thousand Hands wouldn't do that," Chih said. "They are not permitted to close their doors to anyone."

"Oh, their doors are open," said the young man's aunt darkly, sitting slightly behind him. "And if they won't give us water to wash with or food to eat, if they keep insisting we turn our children over to their fosterage, we'll walk right out again, and they'll give us a kick in the ass to send us on our way."

Chih started to say that of course that was not true. The clerics of the Lady of the Thousand Hands served a merciful patron. They were not allowed to hold anything without a plan for how it would serve the world around them. Surely if they had food or water they would offer it, and certainly if they offered fosterage, it was solely to improve lives.

Then they caught the young man's challenging gaze, and they could hear Cleric Sun, *It is not your job to determine the truth, only to determine what they think is true,* and then Cleric Yu-ching, *Do you want people to keep talking to you? Shut up.*

They wrote until their hand was sore and their head swam with names and family ties. The moon was already beginning to set as they left, and they promised to come back the day after tomorrow, when they had their first free half day in a month.

"I think I prefer listening to stories," Chih mused on the way back to the restaurant, and on their shoulder, Almost Brilliant chirped softly.

"I think they would prefer telling them," she said, and she sounded so tired that Chih reached up cautiously to stroke her crest. Almost Brilliant was proud, the oldest in her generation, and inclined to snap, but now she only sighed, leaning into Chih's touch.

"You've been working as hard as I've been," Chih said. "Don't you ever doubt it."

Their walk was mostly uneventful despite the still-crowded streets. On a shortcut through a dark alley, a man melted out of the shadows with a menacing stoop to his shoulders, but something, perhaps Chih's bald head and indigo robe or maybe the fact that they could barely pick up their feet, made him pull back without a sound. Chih was grateful. They didn't have any money on them, but they realized they would fight for the names they'd collected harder than they would have fought for cash.

They had just enough energy to strip off their robe and stuff their notes into their bag before they collapsed onto their pallet in the kitchen. Above them, they heard Almost Brilliant whistling goodnight, and then they were asleep.

Chapter Four

It seemed the most unfair thing that after a long day followed by a long night, Chih woke up before dawn, the heat already pressing down on them, sweat pooled under their arms and between their skin and the thin pallet they slept on. When sleep proved determinedly elusive, they got up and went to wash from the rain barrel.

Almost Brilliant was presumably off scaring the local birds from her own breakfast, but Chih wasn't alone. Little Hulin had gotten up early as well to water some vines growing up along the fence that separated the yard from the alley. She could get the ones closest to the edge, but she struggled to get the ones by the fence.

"Would you like some help?" Chih asked, and when she handed over the jug, they leaned over to make sure all the vines got a proper watering. "What fine healthy plants. I'll admit, I'm not a very good gardener. I have no idea what's growing here."

"Stripe squash," said Little Hulin happily. "They didn't used to be stripey. When I was little-little, they were all green, but now they have yellow stripes on their sides."

"Like tigers," Chih suggested, making Little Hulin giggle with a pretended growl. "You know, Almost Brilliant has some wonderful stories about tigers, like how Ho Thi Thao married the scholar Dieu and how one tiger from Fulan gave up her stripes in exchange for a garnet necklace and became something else instead. You should ask her to tell them to you sometime."

They paused.

"I liked the story you told me about Amo and the floating ghost palace. I've heard similar things before, but never one just like that. I was wondering if you could tell me more about it?"

Little Hulin shrugged, nodded.

"Who told it to you first? Do you remember?"

"Mama's ma did. She had told Little Meng and me lots of stories. When she fell and couldn't work in the kitchen anymore, she would tell us stories all day until Baba told her to stop." Her brow furrowed. "She cried."

"She must have loved telling stories to you and your cousin very much."

"She made good dumplings. She taught Baba. Do you like our dumplings?"

"I do, and I like the good-time stew your mother gave me last night. She said it was from the west like me. Did your grandmother come from Anh like I did? It's all the way across the sea."

She shrugged again, uninterested, and Chih cast around for something that might draw her back in. A soft hooting made them both look over to the fence post where Almost Brilliant had appeared, shaking droplets of water off her feathers like a singing girl wringing out her hair.

"I have a question. Did your grandmother ever tell you where stories came from?"

"From birds. Birds dropped them."

"What birds?" asked Chih excitedly, but Little Hulin only picked up her now-empty jug.

"Birds, like juncos and sparrows and geese and things."

She went back into the kitchen, and Chih turned to Almost Brilliant.

"Stories that come from birds," they said. "Maybe not birds at all, but memory spirits that look like birds. Like you and Myriad Virtues and Cleverness Himself. Like Temperate Above All and Truly Patient. Maybe her grandmother knew a cleric, or even was a cleric. If the years line up, maybe—"

Almost Brilliant gave Chih a stern look.

"That is too many maybes," she said.

Before they could argue, a racket broke out up the street. They jerked their head up, frozen for a moment at the voices raised in anger against the easy early quiet. There was a moment where they hesitated, and then they remembered that Cleric Sun never would have, would have nudged their shoulder as they went by, *Come on, novice, you're going to miss it.*

Miss what? The fight, the story, the chance to see a thing as it happened or the chance to keep it from happening. Chih ran around the side of the restaurant to find a crowd gathering around two women viciously yanking a bucket back and forth between them. One woman was dressed in the now familiar clothing of the refugees from the Verdant Islands, the other was a local. Both were swearing fit to blister stone, and the crowd, mostly other women, some with their own buckets slung over their shoulders, shouted encouragement.

As Chih watched, the refugee woman reached out and slapped the other hard, the sound sending a shock through the watchers. The slapped woman reared back, let go of the bucket, and the crowd surged as Chih shouted. Their voice was lost in the clamor, but Almost Brilliant, puffed up as big as a mammoth melon, whistled shrilly, loud enough that the women fell back with a confused babble.

It was as if a tiger had frozen mid-leap, his claws stretched, his fangs bared. In this moment, Chih felt dozens of eyes on them, and then, almost by magic, they found their voice, or rather, they found the voice of Cleric Yu-ching, who had more than once turned away disaster with nothing more than a joke or a lie.

"Ha Beili! Ha Beili, there you are!"

They had finally recognized the refugee woman, no

woman at all, but the teenager with the excellent monkey call who had seen them hit the water the day before. She jerked back at being recognized, and for a moment, it looked like she was going to run.

Don't do it, Chih thought desperately. Running from a crowd like this would be the worst thing to do. Cleric Yu-ching had told them that: you never ran from a crowd, because then they would chase you.

They let out a careful breath when Ha Beili slunk to their side, leaving the bucket behind so that the local woman could snatch it up again. Ha Beili looked surprised when Chih hooked their arm through hers, or maybe she was just surprised at how tight Chih hung on or how they shivered.

"Ha Beili is helping me with some of my work today," Chih said with a bright smile to the crowd. "Isn't that kind of her? I hardly know anything about the Verdant Islands."

"Dirty, dirty, dirty!" called someone Chih couldn't see, and a titter ran through the mob.

Ha Beili swung towards the crowd, searching out the speaker with murder in her eyes. Against their will, Chih noticed how grimy her hands and her face were, how her clothes hung in lank rags off her body. Well, who wouldn't be dirty after sailing from the islands and up the Ya-lé River?

Cleric Yu-ching had once shamed an even bigger crowd into backing off a pair of brothel boys and handing over donations for Singing Hills besides. Chih didn't think they could swing that, but at least the crowd now looked contemptuous rather than angry. Good enough, Chih thought, and arm still linked through Ha Beili's, they turned to walk up the street. It was one of the hardest things they had ever done, turning their back on a crowd that looked that angry, but they kept their pace slow, their shoulders down from their ears and relaxed.

The women murmured uncertainly, someone said something that made Ha Beili's head snap up, but there were no stones thrown, no further accusations. A quick glance over their shoulder showed the crowd breaking up, some to the vendors, others towards the nearby well. It struck Chih how easy it was for them to do so, how there were so many more things to do in Luntien than to beat a teenager.

Ha Beili started to speak, but Chih shook their head slightly, leading them around the side of the restaurant to the yard.

"That wasn't my fault!" Ha Beili cried out. "It wasn't! I was just getting some water!"

Chih flinched from her strident tone, glancing back into the restaurant where people were still sleeping.

"Please, if you can be a bit quieter—"

"It's not *wrong* to get water! I wanted a fucking bath! I—"

"And whose bucket did you use?"

That was Almost Brilliant, coming to settle down on Chih's shoulder again. Her feathers lay flat against her back and her throat, but she was still agitated, shifting from claw to claw and digging in too hard.

"Huh?"

"The water's free," Chih said, realizing. "No one would begrudge you water to wash here. The bucket belonged to that woman, I think."

"I would have brought it back," said Ha Beili, baffled. "Of *course* I would have brought it back."

"I know," said Chih reassuringly. "She didn't."

Suddenly Ha Beili looked younger, chewing on her lip and on the verge of tears.

"But I would have brought it *back*."

Her voice trembled, and instinctively, Chih folded her into a tight hug as she repeated that she *would* have brought it back, she *would* have. She just wanted a *bath*. Chih rubbed her back firmly like they remembered Cleric Thien doing not so long ago. When Ha Beili was calmer, Chih led her to the rain barrel and let her bathe as they sat close by. They didn't know how Sovann and Phiran would feel about Ha Beili's presence, but they reminded themself that water was free.

After she'd scrubbed herself to glowing, Ha Beili looked better, rolling her eyes when Chih said they were going to walk her back to the temple.

"I'll be fine. Tough as a seven-day goat, that's me."

"I don't know what a seven-day goat is," Chih said with interest, and Almost Brilliant chirped in agreement. "Will you tell us about it as we walk?"

Ha Beili gave Chih a supremely unimpressed look. She knew what they were doing, but she didn't argue, not even when Chih hooked their arm through hers again. It was something a particularly imperious older relative would do in Anh, a demand for support or closeness as well as a claiming. It probably wasn't necessary. Ha Beili probably would have been fine.

Still.

"We have a lot of goats in Muyi. That's where we sailed from, the island of Muyi. The goats, you know, they come from the shipwreck."

"The shipwreck?"

"The big one. The first one?"

When Chih clearly had no idea what Ha Beili was talking about, she sighed, mightily put out, but Chih wondered if she walked taller as well.

"Okay. If neither of you know."

"We don't," said Almost Brilliant, fluttering over her shoulder. "Please. Tell us all about it."

Chapter Five

Okay. So back at the beginning Muyi wasn't an island. She was a god, one of the walkers between the world and its shadow. She was of the fourth generation of gods, so she was closer to us than she was to the air and the darkness. Still she was immortal, and powerful. She wrestled the crocodile that births typhoons. She sailed from the sea to the stars, and she brought back the husband of the great white snake.

Maybe that was why she didn't know what to do when she got lonely. She didn't know how to deal with it like people do. She didn't know how to take a lover, or how to bring her spindle and sit down with the weavers at dusk. She didn't know how to make a baby or to share one. She didn't know how to lure one of the wedge-head dogs down from the highlands to walk in her footsteps. She didn't know how to do anything like that, so day after day, the loneliness grew more at home inside her chest. It hollowed out a place next to her heart, curled up tight at first, but after a while, it started to stretch and to paw at the cage of her ribs. It wanted to come out, and she knew that she could not allow it to do so because it was the loneliness of a god, powerful and bleak and very terrible.

In desperation, she wandered the world with her hands pressed over her chest to keep it in, and at last when she could not bear it any longer, she plunged into the sea and swam out as far as she could.

Ha Beili paused.

"Have you been to Port Yang, on the coast? The place with the purple beach?"

"That's where we came in from Anh," supplied Almost Brilliant. "It was low tide when we docked, and the bones of a green whale had washed up, white against the purple sand."

She had been so pleased to see such a thing, Chih remembered, to be making her own memories rather than merely remembering what she had been told by her parents or held from her ancestors.

"That's where Muyi pushed away from the shore. She kicked at the land and bruised it purple before she struck out for the open sea."

The image touched Chih in a strange way, a goddess who wrestled crocodiles thrusting herself into the waters, her body arrowing through waves to escape a thing she carried within her.

Their musings were interrupted by the glare of a man setting out his baskets of vegetables for the day, and Chih gave him their best serene smile. It made their skin crawl to see a man looking like that at a teenager, but Ha Beili didn't seem to notice, continuing with her story.

Muyi swam all throughout the day, outpacing the dolphin clans and the solitary ladies-in-the-water that tried to keep up with her. When the night came, she turned onto her back and floated, her arms cast wide and her hair floating around her. Inside her, the loneliness beat like a heart, and she asked the sky, *Who can take this away? Who will make me myself again?*

The wind, who was her cousin on her mother's side, took pity on Muyi, and so it blew away the wall of clouds. Now all the splendor of the mid-ocean sky was revealed to her, and so too was the moon at her kindest, fat and round, generous with her light, and she shone down on Muyi without any prudish mountains or trees to get in the way.

Muyi floated in the waters of the ocean, loved by the moon, and for a time, the loneliness went to sleep in the strength her contentment, pulled its claws from the walls of her chest, and gave her peace while she lay in the moon's embrace.

Of course the moon is not always kind. She turns her face towards other lands and other lovers, and as the nights passed, she grew thin and impatient. Muyi cried to her in the dark, and her cries—*Where have you gone, what have I done wrong*—awakened the loneliness that lived in her chest again. It was angry at being so roused, and it struck her over and over again, drawing blood where its sharp claws cut her.

In the darkest part of the ocean, when the moon had turned away from her entirely, Muyi thrashed against the thing that lived inside her. She wanted to live. She wanted to be free of the pain. She wanted her lover the moon back.

She fought, and in her struggle, she whipped the waves up until their peaks touched the stars, until the broad-winged albatrosses drowned in mid-flight. She flooded the ancient city of Queen Harao, breaking the earth it sat upon and sinking it into the sea. Her cries were trapped among the valleys of Laofeng, so loud that the people there still to this day speak with their hands.

With every hour, every moment that passed, she sank deeper beneath the water, and she was on the verge of becoming something else. If she gave in to the thing inside her, she would become bones on the ocean floor. The things that lived there in the darkness, the ones that were nothing but skin spread over soft bones, the ones who lit their own organs to grant some advantage in the blackness, the ones with thin fingers spread out to search for food or for mates, they would eat her. They would rejoice in her flesh, make her a hundred-year feast, make a city in her bones and love each other in places where her eyes and her lips had been.

Muyi did not want to be a dead city for the things that lived in the dark, and so she fought. The loneliness had its hooks deep within her, however, and no matter that she was a goddess, no matter that she was of the fourth generation, she would have sunk beneath the waves if her flailing arms had not encountered a ship.

The treasure ship was called *Where Have You Been?* She was enormous, riding so tall in the water that someone leaping from her deck would find the water below as hard as stone. Her lilac sails were as large as a rich man's fields, and she carried the wealth of a great city to the south, the artists, the scholars, the alchemists, the engineers, and the soldiers, as well as enough gold to buy a thousand palaces and enough cows, goats, chickens, ducks, and pigs to fill their larders.

Muyi seized hold of the treasure ship as tightly as her loneliness had seized hold of her, and it kept her afloat through the long dark night. The timbers groaned, the people and animals wailed, but the ship did not splinter in her arms until the next night, when the moon turned her face back from her other life, a sliver of grace in the night sky. The light pierced the darkness in Muyi's heart, and in her joy, she crushed the treasure ship in her arms. The cry she uttered drowned out the screams of the sailors, the shattering of the wood, the snapping of the masts. She released the wreckage of the ship to embrace the moon again, and her loneliness sank beneath the waves.

For six days, Muyi healed in the light of her love the moon. Then, on the dawn of the seventh day, Muyi looked around in the water, and she saw to her dismay the remnants of the ship that had saved her, the splintered planks, the survivors that clung to them. The sails had ripped clear of the rest, flying all the way to the Sagaran desert to become the tent-palace of the horse queen Marraba, and the great figurehead, a woman with two long snake tails instead of legs, had broken herself away in terror, swimming for the sunrise.

The people had been cracked out of the ship like the yolk from an egg, and those that hadn't drowned clung to the planks of wood, to the bloated bodies of the drowned horses, to the doors and the masses of rigging that floated in the water.

"What have you done to us?" they cried to Muyi. "How will you repay us this pain?"

In sorrow and regret, Muyi rolled onto her back in the water, and she turned herself into an island amidst the waves. Her fingernails became the beaches, her eyes became the lakes. Her breasts and her hips rose into the highlands and her vagina became the red rock caves. Her hair became the kelp beds, the bone necklace she wore became our coral reefs, and so the people of the shipwreck came ashore. The goats, who had survived the seven days of shipwreck by climbing the corpse of a drowned mammoth, came to shore as well, and while cows and pigs and even horses live on Muyi now, the goats were first, and they will not let anyone forget it.

We're the people of the shipwreck, Muyi's people, and in the dark of the moon, we go down to the water to make offerings and dance. We sing to her and we make sure that Muyi knows she will never be so lonely again.

I don't know what's going to happen now. We all left, and soldiers don't dance, and the dead don't sing. I don't know what'll happen. I don't know.

Ha Beili shrugged elaborately, as if suddenly embarrassed.

"Anyway, that's the way we tell it."

During the course of her story, they had come all the way to the temple of the Lady of the Thousand Hands, where an old nun gave them both a suspicious look.

"You were told not to go wandering," she said to Ha Beili. "We told you to stay with your people."

"I wanted to wash," Ha Beili said with a toss of her head. "I did, and now I'm back."

The nun scowled and would have said more, but Ha Beili made a rude gesture at her and pushed by Chih to dart behind the wall, sending Almost Brilliant hooting in surprise into the air to land on Chih's bald head.

"That's a bad one," the nun muttered. "Some of them, nothing more than island trash."

"She's not," Chih said, stung, and the nun shook her head.

"Not all, of course, I'm not saying *that.* But enough of them are, and many of the good ones are related to the bad. They're pirates out there, you know. Thieves."

"She only wanted to wash. They need food and water, no matter who they are."

"And we give it to them, don't we? Clean water, food enough. We're a temple, not a restaurant, we can't be blamed if our regular fare isn't to their tastes, can we? They eat as well as we do."

"And fosterage?" asked Chih, remembering the family they'd spoken to the night before. "Are you offering to relieve them of their children too?"

"I am sure I do not know what you are talking about. We have our hands full right now without taking on new novices. If some families in town have come around offering to foster some likely-looking boys and girls, I hardly see the problem, but that is nothing to do with us. I would think it would be a relief, to parent and child alike. No one wants to live in a camp like that, after all."

The nun gave them a narrow look up and down, and Chih stood up straighter, resisting their first urge to shrink away from an elder's disapproval. They were suddenly very glad their head was freshly shaved and that they wore their cleric's robes. They were sorry there were soy sauce stains on the sleeves.

"You're from Singing Hills."

"I am."

The nun snorted as if that explained everything. Perhaps it did.

"When you actually take it upon yourself to feed someone, to till a field, to mend a seam, to do one simple thing beyond playing with your silly little birds and telling your silly little stories, then you may tell me what's what."

Chih flushed a dull brick red. Cleric Thien would have peaceably asked the nun if something had happened to her that she would say such things. Cleric Sun and Cleric Yu-ching would have cursed her, the former to her face, the latter behind her back. Chih stood there tongue-tied as the nun gave them another assessing look and then returned to sweeping the temple's entry way.

"You shouldn't have let her speak to you that way," said Almost Brilliant on their walk back to the restaurant, and Chih shrugged with irritation.

"I couldn't very well start a fight on the doorstep of her own temple," they retorted, though they had the idea that Almost Brilliant was right.

"She would have said the same thing if she was standing at our own gates. *My* family remembers when the temples to the Lady of the Thousand Hands were nothing but stone cairns set up by the side of the road."

Chih couldn't help a brief laugh at Almost Brilliant's indignation. When they reached up to preen her crest, she allowed them to do so, hooting grumpily.

"That one remembers when Singing Hills was banished by the Emperor of Nails and Storms," she muttered. "She's probably so old she thinks of our clerics as vagabonds with their neixin stowed for safe transport in hatboxes or among racer pigeons."

"Imagine you stuffed in a hatbox. We could line it with my spare under-robe, keep you comfortable for the sea crossing when we go back home next year."

"Pfft, I should like to see you try it."

They made it back to the restaurant in time for their shift. It was even more crowded than it had been before, more and more tourists arriving in Luntien for the end of the festival. The student groups and the families and the tours from the surrounding towns had come in their finest holiday clothes, ready to see the sights, to laugh with their friends, and of course to eat.

"Eat as you go," Bich advised, hipping them out of the way when they were slow at the enormous pot of brown rice. "You're going to be starving by lunch if you don't."

She demonstrated by plucking a strip of raw beef from the cutting board, fast enough to avoid Phiran's flashing cleaver, ignoring his shout of irritation. She dropped it neatly into her mouth and chewed with satisfaction before scooping two perfect mounds of rice onto the waiting plates.

Chih swallowed, because the red strips of beef, marbled with white fat and sliced so thin they were almost translucent, suddenly looked liked the most delicious things in the world, but Phiran shook his cleaver at them menacingly.

"Don't even think of it, cleric! And you Pha thief, I'll cut your damn fingers off, you get them close to my knife again!"

"Ah, maybe you could have when you were young. What was it like, anyway, back when the birds were still dragons?"

Phiran swore viciously, but Bich was already away, whirling her full tray back to the front of the room that was growing more crowded with each passing moment. It was busy enough that lunch never happened for the staff, and the first break that they got was when a clamor of bells and flutes summoned people out into the street. It was the parade, carts decked out in banners and bright swags of fabric with representatives from the local guilds and benevolent societies throwing flowers and candy to the crowd. Almost Brilliant declared that she wasn't getting paid for any of this and went to watch the floats pass by, and before Chih could collapse in a chair, they and Bich were sent to the vendors with a list of supplies.

Chih stared in dismay at the tall pyramids of red mangoes and the piles of scrubbed white tubers, because if they were hopeless at serving food, they were surely even worse at knowing what went into preparing it. Bich, however, merely waved down the vendor and thrust their list into his hands.

"Get us the best," she said imperiously. "This is for Certain Compassion, we'll know if you try to give us the shoddy stuff. And cleric, sit down before you fall down. They're paying you to work, not die."

Chih gratefully sat on the ground in the shade of the fruit vendor's stall, and Bich squatted down next to them companionably, handing them a steamed bun from the cloth bag slung over her shoulder. It was cold, a bit gummy and linty, but Chih devoured it in four bites. They must have looked sad when it was gone because Bich picked out a small fruit Chih didn't recognize from the vendor's stall, twisting the stem off even as the vendor cried out in outrage.

"We're paying for the lot, just add it in!" she snapped. "There are some cheap people in this town."

The vendor growled the same thing Phiran had, *Pha thief,* and Chih gave Bich a curious look.

"Does that bother you?"

"What, that people are so cheap? Yeah, a little."

Bich took a thick flake of blue-gray flint from her bag, shaped with a scalloped sharp edge and a blunted side so she could hold it safely. She split the thick rind on the fruit to reveal an interior of creamy yellow streaked with pink, digging her fingers inside to detach two lobes of the firm pulp and hand them to Chih. They were taut with juice, bursting in Chih's mouth with a slightly perfumed sweetness and a fibrous chew.

"No, that they call you, um, a Pha thief."

"They call me worse than that sometimes. Anyway, there's a big difference between demanding what you're owed, and taking something that someone else needs, and we Pha know it better than they do down here."

She sliced off a bit of the rind, popping it into her mouth and chewing thoughtfully.

"You get used to it, you know? When my family came here, it was worse. *Pha bitch* this, and *Pha whore* that. The Lu folks didn't get it so bad. They'd been driven south by the same storms that did it for my family's farms, but they look more like the Feiyu folks in Luntien. Dress like them too."

She flicked one of her ear spools. This close, Chih could see the delicate floral design that had been incised around the flared edge.

"Ba wanted me and Ma to take these out, have the holes stitched up, but nah. My grandma punched them out for me when I was seven, gave me my first wooden plugs. They're pretty."

Chih suspected they were more than just pretty, but Bich squinted at the street, watching as two boys trotted by carrying armloads of fluttering paper decorations, fringed blue and green garlands designed to be hung up in doorways for luck.

"You asked me about Luntien last night," she said finally. "Well. I've lived here since I was ten. It's fun. The festivals are great, everyone turns out, has a great time. The river means there's always interesting things coming and going. We get lots of acts coming through on their way to the capital up north, and lots of times, they do a show or two in Luntien to prep for the real crowds. I got to see Crimson Bow last year when the Resplendent Sky Overhead company came through. They did *The Tale of Madame Voracious,* which they couldn't do more than two nights in the capital before the city rioted. That was pretty great too.

"The rains take some getting used to. We've got rain back in the highlands, but nothing like this. They scared me at first. Storms like that swept our house away, all our cows and our sheep, but here it just means the year's turning. You'll see it soon. It's rain you can swim in. It's rain you can drown in. It's welcome after all this heat."

"Is Luntien home?"

The question popped out before Chih could stop it. If Almost Brilliant was there, she would have given them such a sharp peck for talking out of turn. Bich only smiled, rising smoothly to her feet and giving Chih a hand up.

"What a stupid question," she said pleasantly. "I live here. Most of my folks are here. They talk about going home, but the storms washed out four generations' work on the terraced fields. Who wants to get that going again? We have houses here. We have jobs. If I wanted a better job, maybe a nice town boy to come sing me songs, I could take out my spools, stop eating my ma's lamb brain curry, but I don't. What do you want me to say?"

Bich laughed as the vendor returned with two heaping sacks of fruits and vegetables for them.

"Stop taking things so seriously, cleric. There's work to be done, isn't there?"

Chih thought for a moment, carefully considering.

"I've never had lamb brain curry before," they said at last. "Is there a place where I could try it?"

This more than anything else made Bich give them a long look.

"Maybe I'll bring some to the restaurant sometime," she said, making no promises. "It stinks if you're not used to it. You can try a bite of mine."

"I would love that."

Chapter Six

The next day, Chih grabbed a cone of rice and crunchy mushroom wrapped in thick green leaves on their way out from the restaurant, eating as they walked. With Almost Brilliant on their shoulder, they threaded through crowds that were even thicker than they had been. The shows and games started early, some never stopped at all from the night before.

Now that they were looking for them, Chih noticed the islanders among the rest, standing out like greenfinches among the local sparrows. They were easy to spot in their long tunics, mostly hauling refuse or providing security at the brothels, but more than that, the crowd eddied around them, as if afraid their misfortune might be catching.

They pulled up short as an islander stumbled from an alley, hastened on his way by a pair of tough-looking men. When he turned to swear at the men who had pushed him out, he got an empty carton used to carry leftovers thrown at him, splashing his long tunic with a garish streak of red gravy.

"Cheating islander trash," one of the men called. "Go the fuck home, see if they like your loaded dice there."

A hand materialized out of the crowd to slap the man upside the head, making him snarl, and shoulders hunched, he slunk away.

"There are too many of them here," Almost Brilliant observed.

"Where are they supposed to be, then?" asked Chih, suddenly angry. It was probably good for a peck; Almost Brilliant hated to be scolded, but she absently preened the side of their head.

"Home, of course. If you asked them that, that's what they would tell you. But what I meant is that a few families would go unnoticed. They'd be unhappy, but they'd be tolerated. As they are, however—"

Almost Brilliant didn't have to continue, because Chih could see it as they walked. The people from the Verdant Islands were obvious, especially where they walked in pairs or larger groups, and while they were mostly ignored, the times when they weren't were hung with threat, with the sense that things could go very bad, very fast.

When they came to the temple, it hit Chih even harder how many Verdant Islanders there were. They were packed in from the wall to the steps leading up the god-house itself, a teeming too-loud mob that stank to the skies, and Chih remembered how desperate Ha Beili had been to get clean. The crowd moved like some great wary beast that had been hurt, terrified to find out how bad it was, how much had been lost.

They are too many, Chih thought, and then their stomach flopped, because no. There could be too little food, too little water, too little money, too little kindness, too little sense; there were never too many people. The archives of Singing Hills were very clear on the matter, but that was difficult to remember in the face of people crammed shoulder to shoulder, children with limbs like spiders sitting on their mothers' laps, men glaring at each other when they weren't gazing off into some middle distance where their lives had not turned inside out.

"Twenty more came off the river," Vang Kao said. "They had money, at least. They bought their own food."

"But surely the temple will feed you all no matter what comes?"

Vang Kao gave them a polite look, and Chih let it go, because the temple would—it would be the same fare the priests and nuns themselves ate, but root mash and water was a punishment unless you chose it.

Once they noticed it, Chih couldn't escape the persistent smell of root mash that sank into the very air within the temple's walls. It was an earthy sour smell, usually alleviated by lard, spices, and onions, of course plain here, and it followed Chih as they made their way between the refugee family groups.

Most of the family heads they spoke to were curt but

polite. They gave their family connections to Chih, allowed Chih to read them back so they could nod with satisfaction or make corrections, and then abruptly, they turned their heads away, indicating that the interview was over. In Anh, it was a spectacularly rude gesture, especially to a cleric, but Almost Brilliant reminded them things were different elsewhere. Singing Hills had records on the Verdant Islands—plants, animals, who had ruled over them and when—but about the islanders themselves, there was precious little. Their absence was a silence that right now screamed at Chih.

Every time Chih thought they had figured out one particular rule in the kinship ties of the Verdant Islands, it seemed they learned there was another rule that should take precedence. In the end, the best they could do was to act as Cleric Sun had always said, as a clear pane of glass where information passed through as perfectly and faithfully as possible.

"And it's not the Verdant Islands. You keep saying Verdant Islands, but you need to stop that," said one ancient man, the head of a household that consisted only of two small twin boys.

Chih looked up, frazzled, fingers cramping and stained with graphite.

"I do?" They couldn't quite a keep a whine out of their voice, and the old man slapped his hand on his knee.

"You do! You ask around for the Verdant Islanders, and we'll say, *Who's that? Who are they related to? Are they those pirates who decorate themselves with glass eyes?* No. I'm Muyese from Muyi. Get it right if you don't want to look like an idiot."

For a moment, Chih was so tired and so hungry that they wanted to tear their notes in half and throw them in the fire. They wanted to shout at the old man that they were doing their best, and if they could just get *one day* where they knew what they were doing, where they weren't working from the time they got up until the time they finally lay down, they would—

They took a deep breath, and managed a smile. It wasn't Cleric Thien's smile, which felt like a warm blanket on a cold night, but it wasn't terrible.

"Of course. I'm sorry, I didn't know that. Here, let me correct it."

They carefully amended their notes, they confirmed with the old man that it was correct, and then they went on. Accuracy above all things, they said at Singing Hills, and that meant above comfort, anger, and pride.

The trouble came as the sun began to set. Almost Brilliant on their shoulder was huddled down into a fluffy ball, not asleep but close, and Chih found themself interviewing a boy they guessed was thirteen or fourteen. His height made Chih think he was older at first, and then they heard his high young voice, saw the way he kept sneaking looks at the other men as if to measure himself against their calm.

"It's all right," Chih said. "I only wish my records to be

accurate so that I can pass them on when I get to Beixia. Come, here, I will read you the cousins on your maternal grandmother's side—"

"Why should you do that?" he demanded, his voice cracking. "I know who my cousins are."

"My cleric is only trying to be accurate," Almost Brilliant offered. "We certainly know—"

"Shut her up," the young man demanded. "I will not talk to witches."

Almost Brilliant immediately settled down close to Chih's shoulder. There were plenty of people in the world who considered the neixin uncanny and unlucky, and Almost Brilliant knew when to shut up. This left it to Chih, who offered the young man a smile that felt false even to them.

"Of course not. Please talk to me. Perhaps you can confirm for me the names of your father's siblings, that should—"

"Why do you want to know that?" the young man demanded. People were turning from their own business to frown at them. "I told you what I told you, I don't *remember* my father's cousins, all right? No one does."

His female relatives were gathered behind him: one tiny child with the shaved head and long forelock worn by baby girls, two girls somewhat older, a woman who might have been an older sister or a very young mother, and a stone-faced old woman who knelt with her hands fisted on her knees. Every time her grandson spoke, her lips went tight. It was like she had to pinch her mouth shut to keep back the answers to the questions Chih was asking, and when her grandson slapped the dirt with the flat of his hand, she visibly jumped.

"I am not talking to you anymore," the young man said, turning away from Chih. "This is stupid, stupid."

Chih started to protest, but Almost Brilliant tugged their earlobe once, whispering urgently.

"Closed doors don't speak. Move on now, and you might have better luck later. And it is time to take a break. You are beginning to look as worn as the North Road itself."

Chih did in fact feel like a track that mammoths had been walking for five generations, and they stepped outside the wall to breathe the clean air and to ease the soft ringing in their ears. They practiced the circular breathing that Cleric Yu-ching always insisted upon, and it helped some.

As they came back into the courtyard, they came face-to-face with the grandmother of the last young man with whom they had spoken.

"It's you!" Chih exclaimed.

The old woman ducked her head, deference personified in the face of a holy cleric. She started to make her way around Chih towards one of the cook fires, but inspired, Chih took her by the sleeve.

"Actually, perhaps you could help me? I am trying to

compile the most accurate records to bring to Beixia, as Vang Kao asked me to do—"

"No," Almost Brilliant hissed. "Stop."

"I am hoping that you might clarify a few things for me. I just need to know the names of—"

Chih flinched as Almost Brilliant exploded off their shoulder, winging her way up to the wall, and only then did they realize that the old woman stood as stiff as a statue, her arm extended as far as it could go while still allowing Chih to hold her sleeve. Her face was stone, and her eyes were full of such a dark offense that Chih let go of her sleeve immediately, stammering apologies.

There was a crowd gathering, their mutterings dire even to Chih's inexpert ear, and a shiver of terror ran down their spine.

"I was only trying to—"

The grandmother turned with great dignity, walking back towards her family's sleeping place, and the islanders closed ranks behind her, their faces as impassable as stone. Chih shrank back, still trying to apologize, but by then Vang Kao had appeared.

His expression was hard to read; Chih thought he must be angry, but when he spoke, his voice was just tired.

"Perhaps you might go enjoy the festival tonight, cleric. We are grateful for your help—"

A low, incredulous murmur ran through the crowd. Chih winced.

"I said, we are grateful for your help, but. Not right now."

It occurred to Chih that they should refuse. Their pay packet might catch up with them as early as the next day. Their time in Luntien was short, and if they were going to create a thorough record, they would need to work steadily. Then their nerve broke, and they turned with as much grace as they could muster, leaving the temple, and trying not to slink when they did it. Beyond the wall, Almost Brilliant came to rest on their shoulder again. They remembered what the boy had said about witches—Almost Brilliant had known not to make things worse. They waited for her to scold them, but she was silent.

"I messed up."

"You did."

"That boy might never speak to me again. His grandmother definitely won't."

"There was never a chance of that, cleric. She's old-line."

Chih jumped. They hadn't noticed Ha Beili following them out, and she lingered in the shadow of the wall like a young tough about to shake them down for cash.

"And I suppose you won't even tell me what old-line means."

Ha Beili held up her hands in mock fear, smirking.

"Ooh, angry, angry."

Chih took a deep breath and then another, because Ha Beili was right. They were angry and embarrassed, and it was Almost Brilliant who came to their rescue.

"I'm not angry," she said pertly, "and I would like to know what old-line means."

"Well, it means no witches, no charms, no dirt magic or water talking, no boys and girls sleeping together, and if the head of the family tells you to leap into the sea, you do it." She rolled her eyes. "The women don't talk outside the house without the men's say so. Pretty hard now when no one has a house."

"You don't seem very fond of them," Chih said, trying for the neutral tone they'd been trained to, and Ha Beili gave them a skeptical look.

"No one smart is," and then grudgingly, "Well. There are more of them now. They came around after my ma died. The women cooked and cleaned for us, and my ba's been talking with the men. Doesn't matter. They're stupid, and stubborn. That old woman would rather drink piss than talk with you now."

"Maybe I could ask Vang Kao to vouch for me, or even send my questions through him . . . ?"

"I am afraid you might make things worse," Almost Brilliant said. "They already aren't happy with us. I think you have to let this one go, at least for the time being."

Ha Beili unexpectedly patted Chih's arm as she ducked back inside. "Go home and get some sleep before you fall over. Who cares about them, anyway?"

The problem was that Chih did. So did Singing Hills, where the archives were punctuated with long, speaking silences, months and years lost to exile or accident or sabotage. Chih felt the shape of the silence they had caused with their carelessness, and they swiped hard at their eyes.

Then because there was nothing else to do, they walked back to Certain Compassion and crawled into their pallet. When they dreamed, it was of people with smooth expanses of skin where their mouths should be, and their eyes were large and reproachful as Chih asked for their family names over and over again.

Chapter Seven

The next night, Bich took one look at Chih's tired face and shook her head.

"You need a night off from all that," she said, gesturing at another bag of crackers she had just given Chih to distribute. "Drop those at the temple and come with me and my girlfriends tonight. We can watch a puppet show, flirt with some tourists, buy some food from the street vendors that's twice as expensive and half as good as what we serve here. You'll love it."

Chih wanted to. Perhaps the world could do without a bad cleric for one night, or at least they could stop being a bad cleric for one night and be someone else. Then they remembered that bad or otherwise, they were the only cleric the refugees had, and they shook their head.

"Tomorrow, then. At least think about it. You're starting to look like a stack of wet rats."

The temptation to follow Bich into the festival crowd

dogged their steps all the way to the temple. They still weren't sure they could bring themself to face another failure like the one from the day before, but then they were past the wall, pulling out their notebook with a sigh of relief. Almost Brilliant, who had been silent the entire way over, whistled softly.

"The first thing you have to do is show up," she said. "I'm glad you did."

It was the same exhausting round it had been before, names and familial connections related in painstaking detail. The young man they'd spoken to the day before refused to have anything to do with them, and a few other families, who Ha Beili had called old-liners, turned away as well. Still, the vast majority of the refugees wanted their family names taken to Beixia, and over and over again, they recited their lineages for Chih to write down.

By the time they finished, names and relations of the entire camp written and remembered, they were humiliated by how close they had come to staying away. They had a notebook full of names: the living, the dead, the lost. It was incomplete, but it was not a silence. If it had been, this particular silence in the record would speak of their cowardice and their doubt, even if only to them. It would scream it.

"You're a cleric, and thus only human," Almost Brilliant said, surprising them. "And you are tired, and that never helps anything."

Chih could have taken a scolding; they honestly might

have preferred it on the chance it would alleviate the guilt that chewed at the back of their mind. Almost Brilliant's understanding just made them feel guiltier. Instead of replying, they wiped their face with their sleeve, pretending they'd been sitting too close to the smoky fires.

Before they were quite ready to walk back to the restaurant, Almost Brilliant sat up straight on their shoulder.

"There's trouble," she said.

There was a crash as a grill that had been propped carefully over a bed of coals was kicked to the brick pavers. People shouted, angry and afraid, and Chih's heart lurched.

By the light of the fire, two figures struggled against each other, the smaller one trying to tear away, the larger one clinging to their arm. When Chih got closer, they saw that it was Ha Beili, her face screwed up and awash with tears, a large man Chih recognized as her father holding her.

They were both shouting, too fast and angry for Chih to catch the words easily, but whatever Ha Beili was saying, her father had had enough. He drew back his hand and slapped her twice on the face, hard enough that she would have fallen if he hadn't still been holding her by the arm.

Chih cried out at the violence, and without thinking, they ran forward as Almost Brilliant tried to call for calm, for everyone to *just wait a minute.* Before they could reach the struggling pair, however, Ha Beili reached up so quickly that Chih only saw her hand flashing in the firelight, and then her father released her with an enraged bellow, clutching at his eyes.

I should be doing something here, Chih thought blankly. *I should be doing something. There's something I should do to calm everyone down, to make everyone understand—*

Understand what? They didn't understand themself, and then Ha Beili rushed by them, nearly knocking them off their feet as she went. Chih would have gone down on their rear, but Vang Kao was there, steadying them with one hand around their upper arm.

"Are you all right, honored one?" asked Vang Kao, and Chih sputtered.

"I am, of course I am, but Ha Beili—"

Vang Kao's face closed like a pair of brass gates, impassable and hard.

"I am ashamed that you had to see such a thing. Please, forgive us."

Behind him, a pair of women, Ha Beili's aunts, Chih thought, rounded on her father, shouting at him, their hands fluttering like birds. He shouted back at them, and now other men were shouting as well, for quiet, for the man to control his family.

"You should go now," Vang Kao said. "We appreciate very much what you have done. If we can repay the favor, if we can ever do you a good turn, we will."

Chih started to say that they didn't need a good turn, Ha Beili did, but Vang Kao herded them out, firm like a shepherd with a particularly silly sheep. When they were beyond the walls, he went back in, and a few moments later, the shouting died down.

"I should have done something," Chih said. Their hands were shaking, and they clasped them together to hide it.

Almost Brilliant made a soft chirping sound. Chih wondered if she was as overwhelmed as they were.

"What should you have done?" Almost Brilliant asked, and Chih had no answer.

When they returned to Certain Compassion, the only person still up was Phiran, stowing an earthenware jug of onions and water spinach under the floorboards to ferment.

"You've been at the temple again," he observed, and Chih's back stiffened.

"I was," they said, sounding defiant even in their own ears, but Phiran only nodded, replacing the floorboards and tamping them down with his bare foot.

"It's good that you're looking in on them. Writing down their stories, whatever it is you do."

Chih couldn't quite hide their surprise, and on their shoulder, Almost Brilliant whistled inquisitively. Phiran gave them a dry look.

"We give to the temple, you know. We want the poor to be safe and fed."

Chih waited, and Phiran considered, then continued.

"My wife's mother, Old Mo, she came in just like they did. She got to work the moment she landed in Luntien, found two jobs, stuck with it. She told us about it sometimes, up before dawn at the printer's, no sleep 'til past dark at the noodle shop. Told us she didn't have any time to cry or miss home, she was working so hard. We won't see her like again."

Chih expected to hear that the Muyese should be working that hard, but Phiran surprised them again.

"She wanted to keep working after she fell. It was like she couldn't stop. We'd find her up in the morning, trying to haul wood for the stove, trying to wrestle the big sides of ribs herself. We kept telling her it wasn't safe, she couldn't do that anymore, she had to wait for us, but she never listened. Said if she didn't work, she didn't know what she would do. We kicked her out of the kitchen, set her up with a chair in the garden, and then she started telling Little Hulin and Little Meng all those stories."

Chih leaned forward eagerly, then stifled a yelp when Almost Brilliant nipped their earlobe. They knew not to ask, they did, but the reminder was a good one. They wanted very much to know what stories Mo had been telling.

"Most of them were fine, Amo and the ghost palace, Princess Bubble. Others, well."

Phiran shrugged uncomfortably.

"Some of them scared the kids pretty badly, and she cried when we made her stop. Old Mo worked hard the moment she got here. Maybe she could have rested some. Maybe she needed to have her stories written down. I don't know. Anyway, past time for me to be in bed. Get some sleep yourself, cleric. It's another long day tomorrow."

When Chih stretched out on their pallet, Almost Brilliant came to perch on the stool by their head, straightening her feathers with her beak as fastidiously as a girl would arrange her skirts.

"We do not guess," she said presently. "It is interesting. It is compelling. It is not proof."

"I never said it was!"

"Remember your lessons, cleric. We do not guess."

"We don't," Chih said. "But we listen to stories. And we tell them. At the end, when we can't cook, can't work, can't go home, maybe all we can do is tell stories."

From where they lay, they could turn their head to look out into the garden, now almost entirely dark. There was no chair there any longer, no old refugee with too many stories. There was no one there at all, not even a ghost.

Instead there was only an absence.

After their shift the next day, Chih ate quickly and was surprised to be stopped by Bich, who handed them yet another enormous bag of crackers before picking up a second bag for herself and a plucked chicken carcass as well, dangling from a string threaded through its head.

"Sovann gave it to me for half off," she said. "We're doing fish tomorrow, anyway."

She walked with Chih to the temple, where they found Vang Kao backed by several large men, talking with a group of locals.

Talking was not quite the right word, Chih thought, their stomach sinking, not when the men behind Vang Kao all bore large sticks and when the men of the town outnumbered them by two to one.

"I am sorry for the thefts, but you will not find the missing goods or the thieves within our camp."

Vang Kao's voice was as patient and smooth as a teacher's with the same expectation of being obeyed. It was, Chih thought, the only thing that kept the locals from simply pushing by him, because they could. They realized, startled, how young the locals were, not much more than boys. They could easily have been Vang Kao's sons or grandsons.

"Then let us in to look," the one who seemed to be in charge demanded. "If you haven't taken anything, you can at least give us that, can't you? Then we'll go away, leave you alone."

"And the next time something is stolen? The next time, and the one after that? If I will not let you come in a fifth time, I will not let you in now."

Chih could see it suddenly, if he allowed them in now. They'd decide it was their right every time something was stolen or even when nothing was, but every time, they would bring the same contempt and suspicion.

The local boys leaned forward tentatively, almost by accident, and they were firmly pushed back by the men with the sticks. No one was struck. No one was pushed down. Chih watched as the Muyese men restrained themselves, even when one was slapped in the face, even when one staggered back from a thrown elbow.

They treated the young locals like cows apt to stampede, and in the end, Chih let out a long breath as the local boys moved on, calling threats and insults behind them to preserve their pride.

"What a lot of idiots. Some people don't have the smarts to go fuck their girlfriends, they have to come out here and do that kind of thing."

Bich's words were careless, but her hand was clamped hard on Chih's arm, her fingers rigid until she forced them loose again.

Vang Kao stiffened when they approached, but he relaxed when he recognized them. He was pleased to see the crackers and the chicken, but despite his thanks, Chih could see how far it wouldn't go given the size of the camp. Beside them, Bich looked around curiously, staring back as unapologetic as a cat when some of the girls stared at her.

"I didn't expect to see you back here. I heard you'd finished with the names and the clans last night."

"I did, and as soon as I make it to Beixia, I'll deliver them to the temple for you. But I was just wondering, ah, Ha Beili."

"I am sorry you had to see that, honored one. It was a disgraceful display."

"Well, actually, I was wondering if she—"

"We appreciate your help, and the food you have brought. You are welcome back here any time. Two more ferries carrying Muyese have arrived from downriver. If you could come back in a few days' time to take their names and relations as well, we would appreciate it. Not tonight, however."

Chih might have pressed the matter, but Bich linked arms with them and, with a nod for Vang Kao, tugged them away.

"That was a get-going if I ever heard one," she said in the plaza before the temple. "I would have thought you knew that."

"Well, of course I do, but that doesn't mean I have to."

"Spoken like a true busybody cleric! Who were you looking for, anyway? Some boyfriend they wouldn't approve of back home?"

"No, a girl named Ha Beili. She got in a fight with her father last night. She took off, and I wanted—"

"Bei-ji's gone."

Both Chih and Bich jumped, looked around and then up to see a boy sitting in the tree above them. Whistling curiously, Almost Brilliant flew up to sit on the branch next to him. When he reached out to grab her, she gave him a brisk peck.

"None of that, I'm a neixin, not a pet," she said sternly. "Now what did you have to say about Ha Beili?"

"She's *gone,*" he said angrily. "She left. She ran away."

His face tried not to crumple, and then he shrugged as if he didn't care.

"She sneaked back last night to grab her clothes and things. She's gone."

Chih made a distressed sound. Bich cocked her head to one side almost exactly like Almost Brilliant would do.

"Should she come back?" she asked shrewdly, and the boy gave her a puzzled look. "I mean, how bad was that fight? She going to get all shit kicked out of her if she comes back?"

The boy looked even more uncertain, and Almost Brilliant whistled, almost gentle.

"Now don't get the idea that I'm a courier service, but what do you want Ha Beili to know?"

The boy hesitated and then he leaned down to whisper his message to Almost Brilliant, who nodded.

"Well, no promises, but if we see her, we'll pass it on."

The boy slid down the tree, bowed belatedly to Chih, and ran back into the temple. Almost Brilliant resumed her perch on Chih's shoulder.

"What did he say?" asked Bich.

"That's hardly for you to hear," said Almost Brilliant. "But we should find her and make sure she's all right."

To Chih's surprise, Bich nodded.

"Right. Well, I'm not spending an entire festival night on this, but I can show you some of the places she might be if she's not too unlucky."

Chih swallowed.

"And if she's too unlucky?"

Bich's smile was faintly ghoulish.

"I'll let you check the corpse cart yourself."

The streets were crammed shoulder to shoulder with locals, with sailors all the way from the delta, with farmers from the highlands, with rich merchants with their swinging sleeves, and with the acrobats who set their poles on the ground and shimmied up them to weave back and forth with the breeze.

Street musicians warred for the best corners to set up, and the festival rang with brassy horns and skin drums. Over it came the cries of the hawkers in front of the brothels, the baths and the taverns, all competing to tell the passersby about the prettiest bedmates, the hottest water, and the strongest grain alcohol.

It was hot, almost hard to breathe with the layer of humidity dropping down on them like a blanket from the sky, and though the festival roared with life and with music, Chih couldn't help a creeping awareness of the ugly rumble underneath. People spoke of the two ferries of refugees Vang Kao had mentioned as a plague descending on Luntien, but they would have feared a plague and gone indoors to let it pass. A plague wouldn't have made them spit in anger, they couldn't drive out a plague with stones and clubs. A plague had no teeth or bones to break, and Chih stared into every face passing by with a growing desperation, hoping to find Ha Beili.

They looked with the actors and the acrobats ("Where every halfway-able runaway goes," said Bich), and they went along the back alleys where the restaurants and taverns kept their scraps-pigs and did their frying and brewing.

"It's the festival season, and these places will take just about anyone. And she can fight the pigs for scraps or beg if she wasn't smart enough to make off with some cash when she ran away."

"You seem to know a lot about the business of running away," Chih said curiously, getting themself a warning peck from Almost Brilliant.

"Sure do," Bich said. "And it looks like you don't."

"Well, no, I—"

"What's your plan, anyway? You gonna shave her head and make her a cleric like you?"

"That's not how anything works and I. I just want to make sure she's all right. Maybe I can. I don't know."

Bich stopped in the middle of the road, turning to Chih and forcing a man carrying an enormous tray of turtle-shaped pastries to pivot around her with a curse.

"Maybe you can get her to come home like a good girl?" she asked, her voice overly mild.

"No, that's not my job! I'm not that kind of cleric—"

Chih yelped as a stout short woman wearing only a loincloth shouldered by, a smaller woman behind her carrying a banner for the Wrestling Moon Bear of the Utar Steppes.

"Get out of the thoroughfare, the both of you," scolded Almost Brilliant. "You'd never catch me being so inconsiderate if I had to walk like you do."

They stepped between two food tents, fried fish on one side and fried sweet dough on the other, and Chih shook their head.

"I told you, I just want to make sure she's all right. That she's safe. And all right, maybe that means going back to her family. It's not exactly safe out here for a Muyese girl."

"It's not safe anywhere. I bet it's not safe to wander the world with a shaved head and robes that say you're not allowed to carry weapons, either, but here you are."

"And maybe I shouldn't be!"

Almost Brilliant hooted in astonishment, fluttering up to the edge of the awning. Chih was suddenly aware of how light their shoulder was without her, and the rush of emotion that brought made them queasy.

It all came out, everything from losing their purse to the mess at the docks to the grandmother who wouldn't speak to them and the Muyese—*not* Verdant Islanders. It was all mistakes strung one after the other like beads on a string. The words burned their throat, this felt horrible, was this what it felt like when people gave them their stories? No wonder no one wanted to do it.

By the end, Chih was panting, raw as if they had been scraped inside and out. Bich gave them a gentle slap on the shoulder.

"I can't help you with that," she said, shaking her head, "but I will say I've seen you work, and I think that it will be a good long time before you're as good at waiting tables as you are at writing down stories. Let's go find your girl."

Chih followed Bich back into the crowd, and Almost Brilliant came to perch on their shoulder again. Chih wondered if Almost Brilliant was going to scold them for their outburst, but she was silent, her head twisting back and forth to take in the tumult of the festival. Her weight, slight as it was, comforted them, and they reached up to preen her crest.

Chapter Eight

Chih slept poorly that night. They dreamed that they were on a ship, not on the deck as they had been for their crossing from Anh to Feiyu but in the hold. It was dark and close, too hot and too cold by turns, and they couldn't straighten their arm out without touching someone who did not want to be touched.

"I want to go home," they said to Almost Brilliant, huddled under their apron. "I just want to go *home.*"

"I see, I see," said Almost Brilliant, cocking her head left and then right. "Where's that?"

Chih woke up thinking about the answer, and for once, they'd woken up when everyone else did, lining up for their chance at washing water, getting a bowl of still-steaming pork and crayfish dumplings and slices of pickled radish. They sat on the crate that had apparently been designated as theirs, and they ate the dumplings, chewing mechanically at first, and then more slowly as they considered. They picked up the last one from their bowl between their chopsticks. They thought of what people brought from home when they had to leave in a hurry. They thought of the old man who wanted them to be sure they got the story right, who he was, what he was called.

"I think," they said slowly, "I am going to marry this dumpling."

They spoke into one of those natural gaps in the conversation when everyone else was paused, and their words were as clear as if they had been struck onto a bronze plaque. A ripple of laughter ran through the group, and Bich slapped their shoulder.

"Your order's going to kick you out, you keep talking like that, and then where will you be? You can't support your fat little bride by waiting tables, that's for sure."

"I'll learn some other trade," Chih said earnestly. "I'll geld pigs. I'll go door to door selling pamphlets full of folk cures from the northern confederation. I will provide this amazing dumpling with the finest luxuries money can buy."

"Foolish," Sovann sitting nearby proclaimed, but Chih noted that she had a pleased look on her face.

"Love makes me foolish, especially when it comes to Feiyuese food, which I've never had before I came here."

"Huh, shows what you know about food and what you know about love," Sovann retorted. "Can't you tell, cleric? That dumpling's as western as you are."

"Is it?"

"Use your tongue, go on, tell me what you taste."

Chih bit the dumpling in half, rolling the bite around their mouth. Most of the staff had moved on from Chih's silliness, talking about the acrobats they'd gone to see the night before, but Sovann sat with her chopsticks raised, reminding Chih of a statue of one of the Perfected with her hand lifted in the teaching pose.

"Well, there's pork and crayfish, of course."

"Ha, it's not supposed to be crayfish. It's supposed to be this kind of bony fish that we don't have here."

"Liao-liao!" Chih snapped their fingers. "It's this little fish that's all over the place in the west. You can go down to the streams and catch enough for dinner in your scarf."

"Right! That one. It's so small that you can eat it bones and all. My man and I, we went to Anh for a trip right after we were married, and I got to try some. What else can you taste?"

"Fish sauce and garlic. Something else sweet, not just the pork?"

"Black sugar. We cook it down from sugarcane juice, takes forever, but it's worth it. See how you can't taste any bitterness at all? That's because we're careful not to burn it."

"How long do you cook it?" Chih asked curiously, and Sovann shook her chopsticks at them, mock scolding.

"Don't think I don't see you with your little notebook, running around, keeping track of everything. No one needs to know how we cook our food!"

"You're right, I'm sorry. I can't cook at all, I just know how to eat. So there's black sugar, and black pepper and white pepper, I think? And . . . wood ear mushroom for the crunchy bits and cardamom? Is that what tastes like flowers?"

"You're a good eater," said Sovann with approval. "Yes, that's right. We're the only ones who use the wood ear mushrooms around here, and I don't mind who knows because they're a pain to get. We have a man in Port Yang, and *he's* got a cousin over in Anh, and they're the ones who get it for us."

"Lucky!"

"Luck, nothing, that was hard work finding those men. My mother, who came to work at this restaurant and eventually bought it out, she knew folks back in Anh who would send it to her directly, but even then, she was really exacting. She'd make them send her a dozen samples of mushrooms from different forests, and she'd soak them all in water before tasting them, raw and fried and stewed. She said the only mushrooms that were right for this dish were from this one region, the Sif-something, but she couldn't get them anymore."

"The Cifu forest!" Chih cried, clapping their hands in recognition. "I know where that is! That's close to the Singing Hills."

"Yeah, that's right! That's where the mushrooms taste right, she said."

"The Cifu forest was declared a national preserve,"

Almost Brilliant commented from the rafters. Chih hadn't noticed her coming in. "Harvesting from it these days requires a license."

"Yeah, and your ma wasn't going to get any kind of license," said Phiran, going by and tweaking Sovann's apron strings. She made an impatient noise and, faster than Chih expected, reached out to pinch his arm with her chopsticks, making him yelp theatrically.

"Shut up, we're not talking about that, we're talking about mushrooms."

"Old Mo was a bandit," Phiran continued, rubbing his arm. "On the run from the west where she stole mushrooms."

Sovann opened her mouth to scold him, but one of the second cooks, a man as short as Chih was but half again as broad, laughed.

"Old Mo? No, she was no bandit. She was a nun, you know. Fell in love with a married nobleman, and became a nun for love of him."

"Foolishness!" exclaimed Sovann. "If she was a nun, why'd she marry my father, huh? Explain that."

"Well, that one's going to marry a dumpling. Who knows what clerics get up to?"

Sovann stood up decisively, clapping her hands to shut off the stream of ridiculousness.

"My mother wasn't a nun or a bandit or a pirate or any other silly thing you're thinking of. What she was, however, was a good cook, and she never imagined her kitchen full of useless gossips when there was work to be done. Now everyone get to work!"

Chih sighed, standing up, but Sovann stopped them briefly.

"Ma was a good woman," she said emphatically. "I don't want you to get it in your head she was some kind of criminal."

"Of course not."

"She was from the west. She came over young during some trouble sixty years ago, but a lot of people did."

Almost Brilliant fluttered down to Chih's shoulder.

"Sixty years ago, that was during the reign of the Emperor of Nails and Storms. A large number of people fled, most of them poets and scholars and teachers."

And clerics, Chih didn't say. Singing Hills' habit of keeping their own records and not surrendering them upon imperial demand had gone very poorly with the Emperor of Nails and Storms.

"Yes. A lot of them came here to Feiyu. Not many stayed in Luntien, but some did, and that was my mother. She got right to work, first with printers, and then she worked here for eight years before she bought it outright. She married my father, and they worked hard all their lives."

She paused.

"My mother made a life for herself here. She wasn't like

the islanders who stole your purse and fight in the streets all night. I want to make sure you write that down."

"I will certainly record what you have told me," Chih said, stifling an urge to protest how unfair it was. Whether due to tyranny, flood, fire, or war, people displaced were people displaced, but they weren't sure they could convince Sovann of such a thing. They weren't sure they could even make an attempt without losing the progress they had made.

Sovann turned to greet the delivery of a crate of live chickens, but Chih decided to press their luck.

"A lot of the people who fled Anh during that time were well educated. Scholars, advocates, writers. Was your mother involved with something like that?"

Sovann was counting out the chickens, wringing their necks before throwing them onto her block for beheading and then scalding.

"Hm? Oh, yes. When she died we found boxes full of papers stuffed underneath her bed. We all know how to read, of course, my mother would have died of shame if any of us couldn't, but we didn't have much use for it. The priest from the temple offered to take the lot." She frowned. "Are you standing still in my kitchen when customers have started to come in?"

"Absolutely not," Chih assured her, tying their apron on.

"That worked," Almost Brilliant murmured against Chih's ear. "I didn't think you were going to get that from her."

"As it turns out, you learn more being wrong than you do being right," Chih said, and they went to greet the chapwoman with her rack full of pamphlets strapped to her back, hungry and hoping for some eggs on rice.

Chapter Nine

They spent another fruitless night looking for Ha Beili, finally checking the corpse cart as Bich recommended. The sole occupant was a skinny person in a green robe, too tall and skinny to be Ha Beili. They had fallen, their head an irregular shape, and Chih murmured a soft prayer for the dead before backing away.

Sometime after midnight, Chih gave up and went back to Certain Compassion, where they found that they couldn't sleep. They tossed and turned until the night gave up to the day, and in the gray dawn, they made their way back to the temple of the Lady of the Thousand Hands. It was early enough that the camp wasn't stirring yet, and they picked their way through the tents to the god-house itself, whose threshold they had not properly crossed yet.

They removed their sandals and cleansed their feet, their hands, and their face, and when they were done, they sprinkled a scanty handful of water as well over Almost

Brilliant, who took her place on Chih's shoulder with the raised crest and the perfect posture she affected when they were around other orders.

The god-house was tall and spacious, the space dominated by a statue of the Lady of the Thousand Hands herself. She sat on her sacred lotus, one hand holding a fluted vial of sacred water, the other welcoming all into her mercy. This statue, like so many of the ones Chih had seen in their travels, bore a faint smile on her plump carved face, and Chih couldn't help an answering smile of their own as they knelt down in the shadowy rear of the hall to bow three times in respect.

It was early enough that no one was about except an elderly nun, her head shaved to a nicety, her ocher robes bearing the comfortable, lived-in softness that came from years of use with only one day in five to spend in ease. Her prayer beads were dark and smooth, and even now she fingered them absently as she went to remove the altar settings from the closed cupboard off to one side.

"Can I help?" Chih asked, and then they jumped when the nun yelped, the metal bowls hitting the ground with a resounding clang.

"I know how to greet clerics from across the world, how to offer them the respect and honor that is their due, and none of them involve scaring them to death," Almost Brilliant muttered in their ear, and Chih ignored her as they hurried forward to gather up the bowls.

"Yes, you might as well bring them over and set them

up since—" She took a closer look. "You're a cleric. And a baby."

"No! That is. No. I am Cleric Chih, of the Singing Hills abbey, and this is my companion, Almost Brilliant."

"Greetings to the one who follows the eight-fold way, who finds wealth in sunlight and sustenance in kindness," Almost Brilliant said, and then she deflated when the nun snorted.

"It's too early in the day for *that.* You're the recorders from Anh, aren't you? The ones who had such a great deal of trouble with the emperor there."

"We are," said Almost Brilliant, regaining some of her dignity. "We chose to leave our home during the reign of the Emperor of Nails and Storms, seeking lands that might love our talents better."

The nun shrugged. "Well, no one likes a busybody. Here, lend a hand, cleric. Stack these up over there, and then come back for the incense."

Relieved to have clear directions for once, Chih helped the nun set up the altar to the Lady as well as the half-dozen or so subsidiary altars to some of the local deities who shared her home.

As they worked, Chih thought of the expulsion of Singing Hills from Anh, which Almost Brilliant had described in the most polite way. When they were very young, they remembered sitting with their best friend Ru to listen to ancient Cleric Shio talk about the day a boy had run up from the Red Road to tell them that soldiers were coming, the emperor's threats realized at last, and the flurry of panic as everyone had rushed to save what they had never really thought would be threatened. The neixin, Almost Brilliant's grandparents and great-grandparents, had taken flight, some starting the long sojourn to the sister abbey in Tsu, others harrying their human partners to hurry, hurry, hurry, there was no time anymore.

"Earnest in All Things and I ended up all the way out in Fulan, where we stayed with my sister. I tell you, they didn't know what to make of us out there, always asking for the history of this or the story behind that. They were kind to us, but we never stopped waiting to go home. When the Emperor of Nails and Storms died, when his son the Emperor of Pine and Steel allowed some of the other orders to return, we were ready. And when word came back that the Empress of Salt and Fortune had taken the throne, I was one of the many who wrote to her, explaining who we had been and how we served."

Cleric Shio had smiled, showing off the sharp notch in their front tooth. Their sister's family mended sails for a merchant fleet, and they'd spent their years in exile pulling a steel needle through thick canvas with their teeth.

"And then one fine day, I got up and bid my sister goodbye, thanking her for her hospitality. Then I and Only Sorrows, Earnest in All Things' son, boarded a ship, and then we rode in a cart, and then we walked, and finally, we came home."

Home, Chih thought with a sudden unexpected pang,

and they shook it off to pay more attention to the altars they were tidying. There was a stone statue of a dancing dragon, balanced beautifully on one delicate claw, and a wooden statue of a woman holding her robe open to show the dog snarling between her bare legs. Beside them was a clay statue of a chubby little boy in a loincloth, one hand raised in the welcoming gesture, the other hand holding a small round ball.

"That's Little Panuk," said the old woman, spying their interest. "He's a terrible rascal."

"Not a god?"

"Well, he is that too. He's the son of an old soldier and the Ya-lé River. A warlord came to Luntien to take it for himself, and he would have done it if he hadn't been rude to Little Panuk. Every rock that scamp threw grew enormous in the air and crushed a battalion underneath it, and that's why we have the rock formations to the west of town. Also why we're so polite in Luntien. But I will still ask you why you've come. I doubt it's to help an old nun with her duties."

"I wanted to ask about a donation that was made to your temple a while ago. A priest from this temple oversaw the death of Mo, who owned the restaurant Certain Compassion. I was told that afterward, the family donated some papers here. Is it possible that the temple retained those papers, and if so, could I see them?"

The nun's face creased with unexpected dread.

"Oh dear, I'm not sure about that."

"Honored one, we are not mere tourists," Almost Brilliant said. "Singing Hills abbey lies under the protection of no less than the Empress of Salt and Fortune herself. Our records go back to the—"

"It's not that at all. You should come with me."

She led them out the back of the temple, where there were small buildings that presumably held the living quarters for the nuns and the priests and a large building set against the rear wall. The nun unbarred the door for them to reveal the interior, where the space was carved into narrow aisles lined with crate after overflowing crate, stacked up to the ceiling, and dim enough that Chih had to squint.

"You are certainly welcome to the documents if you can find them," she said. "We inherited this mess from the last head priest, who was likely the one who saw to the owner of the restaurant. He was a good man, a very good man, but he came from Haiyang. Too much war, too much famine, and it'll make you a little. Well."

A glimpse into one of the crates revealed piles of dusty burlap, former feedsacks with the stitches ripped out to leave them squares of cloth. It was the kind of thing that could conceivably be useful in the right time and the right spot, but the Lady of the Thousand Hands only knew when that might be.

"I understand," Chih said, gazing around them. They did. They were coming to realize how much one could lose thanks to a little bad luck. Being from the wrong side of an ocean, the wrong bank of the river, the wrong side of an argument, was all it took to change things forever, and you never knew when a pile of burlap might make all the difference.

"If you really want to dig in, I think the most recent things the priest stashed in here are located in that corner," she said, pointing. "You could start there, if you wished."

"I do. I have some time before I need to be at work, but I can come back tomorrow morning as well, I think."

"That would be splendid. This place has needed someone to give it some semblance of order for years. As a matter of fact, I was wondering . . ."

She hopefully offered Chih a bound ledger that had been tucked into a niche in the wall. It was neatly ruled, and the first few pages contained someone's brief attempt to bring some order to the chaos in the form of an inventory.

"That's not organized at all," Almost Brilliant exclaimed with some indignation, and Chih smiled, folding the book under their arm.

"I'd be happy to see what I can do."

And oddly enough, they were. It wasn't that they were incredibly eager to go sifting through what looked like a generation's worth of vaguely usable junk. It wasn't even that they loved the art of cataloging. Some of their friends from home did, but Chih themself much preferred fieldwork, following the senior clerics around on fact-finding missions and study trips.

This—the cataloging, the organizing—was the work they knew how to do. They knew how to create categories and then to sort things into them, how to write it all down so that someone had at least a fighting chance of finding that information if they should need it. It was soothing and comfortable, but they realized they really didn't *like* it. They could do it, and they would, because it was work that needed to be done, and it would help them figure out more about the truth of Mo and the birds that dropped stories, but it was tedious and exacting, and beyond the satisfaction of carving a tiny bit of order out of the chaos, it was deadly dull.

As they walked back to the restaurant, Almost Brilliant tweaked their collar with her beak.

"What's got you looking so thoughtful?"

"I was thinking of Cleric Sun, and how they said that easy was only something you knew how to do. Easy's just experience and practice and time put together until you don't notice them any longer. One day, something you couldn't dream of doing a year ago is something you can do without thought, and you think it must have always been that way, but that's not true."

"Did you think your note-taking was much improved in there? Because I was looking over your handwriting, and—"

"Ha, no. But maybe I'm not as bad a server as I was a week ago, and maybe I'm a better cleric than I was a week ago too."

They returned to the restaurant on time, but with the festival entering its ninth day, their patrons were demanding entrance early. Chih and Bich had to take their meals in bites from the large tray of food left in the back for everyone to grab from. Rather than the hodgepodge of leftovers and scraps that Chih might have expected, it was at least as good as and possibly better than what they were serving, fresh discs of steamed bread kept warm under a woven wicker cover, a bowl of grilled vegetables and chicken nearby to stuff in them, and a dish of spiced yogurt sauce to top it all.

"Can't have you all keeling over, and the gods know how Little Bich will cry if she has to be hungry even a day," said Phiran, and Chih grinned, eating a piece of bread stuffed with cumin-simmered chicken in five bites.

It was a busy day, and while it never quieted from opening until Bich and Sovann shouted the last stragglers into the street, it at least went quickly.

"Did you ever find your girl?" Bich asked as Chih sat flat on the floor, gratefully draining their bowl of root vegetable and cabbage soup.

"No, unfortunately. No sign of her at all."

"Well, I have a few hours before my friends and I head down to see the pretty boys compete in the night-diving contests. Come on, eat up. I haven't got forever."

Chih was grateful that Bich was so decisive. They, on the other hand, were running on several nights of rather terrible sleep, and left to themselves, they probably would have just bleated for Ha Beili from the restaurant steps and been startled when she did not materialize.

When they were this tired, the festival took on a hallucinogenic aspect, something at once too close and strangely far away. When Chih asked a pork floss vendor about Ha Beili, the woman's tray of fluffy fried dried pork seemed momentarily to be a part of her, growing into her hands and up her arms like a luxuriant ruddy pelt.

I wonder if her people groom and style it, Chih thought haphazardly. *I wonder if there are restrictions on whether they can grow the sweet kind or the spicy kind.*

"Okay, cleric, you're worthless. Time to go home."

Chih jumped.

"No, I'm fine," they insisted. "I want to keep looking."

"What we want and what we can do are two very different things," said Bich with a startling amount of diplomacy. "I guess you had no idea that you said that out loud, huh?"

"Eh?"

Chih became aware that the pork fluff vendor was looking at them with wary concern, and they flushed, giving her an abbreviated bow.

"I'm so sorry—"

Bich got them firmly turned around and pointed in the direction of the restaurant.

"You're sorry, all right. Go on, get some sleep. I'm going to catch up with my friends, and I'll even ask for your Ha Beili when I go see the night-diving, all right?"

Almost Brilliant perked up.

"Night-diving! That's when they jump into the dark water after brass tokens, isn't it? I have a cousin who told me about night-diving. I think I would like to see it for myself."

She fluttered from Chih's shoulder to a nearby post, looking at Bich expectantly, who laughed.

"All right, then, me and the bird are headed off to have some fun, and you can go home and get some sleep. We'll bring you back some sweets, all right?"

Chih thanked her, trying not to sound too sullen about being sent to bed as if they were a child. The truth was, however, the minute they started thinking about their pallet, they could think about nothing but, how it would feel to lie down and close their eyes, to be utterly blameless until they woke up in the morning.

Chih started the walk back to Certain Compassion, threading their way through the crowd. It was as if the entire world had come to Luntien in the final days of the festival, and twice they had to backtrack to avoid streets that were entirely blocked off, one by a street theater, the other by an ox-cart crash. Two of the oxen had taken exception to one another, bellowing their rage among the splinters of their carts, and Chih circled around the people looking to get away from them and the people looking to lean in closer and place their bets. They were halfway to the restaurant when they came around the corner straight into a gout of fire. They shrieked, reeling back as someone grabbed their clearly inebriated fire-eater, shouting a *sorry* as they dragged him away.

They would have gone straight to the ground if they hadn't managed to grab on to the person who walked into them. Chih stopped in their tracks and stared.

"Ha Beili!"

Ha Beili, a bag slung over her shoulder, drew back in surprise. Her face was shiny with sweat, and her hair hung in untidy hanks around her face, but she looked all right, no worse for the wear than when Chih had seen her last.

"Cleric? What are you doing here?"

"I've been looking everywhere for you! I was—"

"Why?"

"Um, I was worried, and everything happened so fast, and—"

"I'm fine, as you can see, and now I should—"

"And Almost Brilliant has a message for you from your brother, I think, and—"

"Great, I should—"

"Are you all right? Where have you been? I mean, do you have food? A safe place to sleep? I can—"

"Look, I really need—"

"Stop, thief!"

The cry went up behind them, and Ha Beili cursed, taking off at a dead run. Chih, who hadn't let go of her arm, was yanked along for a few paces, and then fell into step, running beside her. Out of the corner of their eye, they saw the crowd parting around a trio of angry people all wearing shin-length butchers' aprons, garishly streaked with blood.

"What's happening?" they gasped. "Why are they calling you a thief?"

"Oh, why do you think!"

Chih took Ha Beili's hand as they ran, dodging into the mob of dancers. A band, drummers, horn players, and an unnervingly large and therefore loud steel guitar had taken over half the street, and Chih and Ha Beili rocked with the motion of the crowd as it jammed and then flowed with the rhythm. Their one consolation was that the people after Ha Beili were likewise hampered, and Chih hissed as someone stepped hard on their foot.

"Whatever it is, we can give it back!" Chih pleaded.

"It's a suckling pig, and I already sold half!"

"Then the money! You can give them the money. I can talk to them for you, it'll be fine."

Abruptly, the crowd spat them into an emptier spot, and without letting go of Chih's hand Ha Beili took to her heels again, her bag bouncing on her shoulder.

"Where are we going?" When Ha Beili didn't respond, they understood the answer was that she didn't know.

I need to get her to stop. The more you run, the more they chase you, and the longer you make them chase you, the angrier they are going to be when they catch you.

The sensible thing would be to let go of Ha Beili's

hand, and in doing so to let go of the trouble chasing her. Chih, terrified, gripped Ha Beili's hand tighter and matched their steps to hers, the festival turning to a blur of faces and colors and fires that whipped past them. Every time it looked as if they might have gotten away from their pursuers, the cry went up behind them, louder every time with more voices to raise it, and they were running again.

Chih was never a good runner, stable and sturdy rather than nimble. Somehow, probably through the power of sheer terror, they kept pace with Ha Beili, and when they came to a familiar intersection, they tugged her up the street.

"Thousand Hands," they gasped. "We can go to the temple, they can't do anything to you there, it'll be safe there."

They caught a glimpse of Ha Beili's dark face, sheened with sweat, her eyes rolling and showing the white all around. She had been running too long, gone longer without food or rest. Chih had no idea if she understood them, but she followed where they led, darting between two large women carrying two slender women on their shoulders with a banner stretched between them. Behind them, more people had joined the chase, their shouts ominous and ugly.

The temple is safe, they wouldn't violate the temple grounds, bring violence past the walls. No one ever has. It's safe. It's safe.

Chih hung on to that thought as they panted up the street, panic running out as they came to the plaza before the temple.

It struck Chih belatedly that there were more people in front of the temple than there should have been. The temple of the Lady of the Thousand Hands was set a bit back from the thoroughfare, and there were more interesting things to see and do beyond it. The street before the temple should have been relatively clear, and Chih realized with a surge of dread that it was not.

It seemed as if most of the people from the camp were out in front of the walls, men and women of course, but also children and the elderly. Vang Kao was arguing with one of the nuns, the entire camp had turned out to watch, and one man split himself apart from the rest, his face contorted with anger.

"Ha Beili!"

Ha Beili skidded to a hard halt, drawing Chih up with a jerk, not letting go of their hand. They had a moment to see that her dread of her father was at least equal to that of the people chasing her, and then, abruptly and finally, it was too late.

The people chasing them caught up, and it was far more than the men Ha Beili had robbed. Instead it was a cataclysm of people from the festival. Chih thought they recognized one of the dishwashers from Certain Compassion as well as a woman they had served earlier that night.

She had fried chicken in chili sauce, Chih thought wildly, throwing out an arm to ward off a large man who was nearly on top of them.

"Everyone, stop, please, just a moment!" they shouted, and that was all they could get out before, with a feeling like lightning striking the ground, the two crowds came together in an explosion of violence and force.

The only light came from the lanterns sat high on the temple walls, and by their light, deceptively soft, deceptively peaceful, the people below howled and lashed out, fists flying, feet kicking. Someone caught Chih by the sleeve, intent on dragging them off their feet onto the ground, and Chih, renewed terror surging through their body, pulled back out of their grasp. They won themself free but then they stepped straight into a dizzying blow from someone's outflung arm.

Pain exploded across their cheek, and Chih shouted with pain, lurching back and coming shoulder to shoulder with Ha Beili again, but only for a moment. They caught a glimpse of Ha Beili's face, blank and terrifyingly numb, and then two men caught her up between them and thrust her to the ground. When she tried to twist onto her belly, one stepped on her shoulder to pin her in place, and the other one drew back his foot to kick her.

Chih threw themself forward, and in that moment, they were somehow beyond their skin while pressed fully to its limits. There was a roaring in their ears, their heart beating faster than a neixin's wings, the word *no* repeated over and over again between their temples.

The word *no* was so loud it obliterated everything else, and then, just as Chih crashed into the man who was going to kick in Ha Beili's ribs, something in the sky roared in answer.

Thunder boomed and lightning cut the air, briefly illuminating the plaza like it was day. That was the only warning anyone got before the sky let go of the rain it had held for half the year. Chih was instantly soaked to the skin, and then they shouted as something very hard struck their shoulder.

For a moment, they thought someone had tagged them with a stick, one of the refugees or one of the festivalgoers, it could have been either in the darkness after the strike, but then another blow came, this one stinging their fingers to numbness and they felt the cold of it and could make it out on the ground as well: a hailstone almost as large as their own fist, and all around them, people started to scream.

Chih was moving before they decided to. The two men had fled, and Chih hauled Ha Beili up by the arm.

"I'm not going to the temple," Ha Beili said immediately, and suddenly Bich was there, Almost Brilliant on her shoulder.

"Sure. This way, and run fast, because I am not getting brained by the gods for dancing when it wasn't my turn to do so."

Chih resolved to ask Bich about that saying later, but then they were running, all three of them, around the corner and away from the crowd, some of whom were getting under cover in the temple, the rest scattering like birds under thrown stones.

They didn't have to go far. Someone had set up some makeshift stalls in an alleyway, and they huddled underneath its shelter with a quartet of slate-blue oxen, wincing when the hail struck the roof and bounced off.

Chih carefully pulled one of the hailstones under the shelter with them and showed it to Almost Brilliant, back on their shoulder and turning her head forward and back.

"How extraordinary. How terrifying," she murmured. "To think the sky could throw such things."

"Little Panuk," Chih mused, thinking of the boy on the altar. "I guess he thought we were being rude." They wondered if anyone would write that story, that it was the intervention of the god who had saved the day, or if anyone would even know that the day had needed to be saved. Then they understood. There'd be no silence over what had just happened save one they created, and they weren't in the business of silence. They never would be.

Experimentally Chih licked the hailstone, tasting brackish water, and then they handed it to Ha Beili, who gratefully pressed it to her swelling cheek. She looked smaller than she ever had, leaned back against the wall of the makeshift stable, and they would need better light to see what injuries she might have taken. She glared when she caught Chih looking, and Chih turned to Bich and Almost Brilliant.

"I thought you two were going to the night-diving."

"We were, and then someone was talking about some islander girl who had gone stealing pork from butchers. I thought it might have been the one you were looking for, so me and the bird looped back to tell you. I guess you found her on your own."

"I was hungry," Ha Beili protested, and Bich nodded peaceably.

"Sure. Next time, do it better so the whole damn town doesn't drop on your head."

It startled a laugh out of Ha Beili, so sweet and startlingly young that Chih couldn't bring themself to do their duty and suggest that stealing was not the preferred method for dealing with hunger.

They leaned against the wall and closed their eyes. After a moment, Almost Brilliant fluffed herself into a round ball and nestled against their neck between their ear and their shoulder, and they drifted off together to the sound of the hailstones striking their clumsy roof.

At some point, Bich got them up and moving again through streets drowning in rain. The hailstones had stopped, but the streets were as empty as Chih had yet seen them, no one wanting to test their luck unless they had to. Chih hadn't been feeling particularly lucky lately, but they made it to Bich's house without incident.

Bich lived in two rented rooms behind a raw-fish restaurant with her mother, her younger sister, and her toddling niece. Ha Beili produced half a suckling pig from her bag, and as Bich's sister cleaned her face and made distressed noises over the big chip out of her front tooth, Bich and her mother cut slivers from the pig, thin enough to cook fast on the sizzling pan over the fire. These they rolled up with cold white noodles into lettuce leaves, dipping the whole thing into a dark sticky-sweet sauce with each bite. It was very good, and Chih managed two rolls before they nearly nodded to sleep straight into their plate. Bich's mother noticed, and after shooing Bich, her sister, and Ha Beili into the other room to continue their talk, she rolled out some thin mattresses that covered the floor from wall to wall. They were stuffed with wool and quilted over every inch, monstrously comfortable, and Chih stifled a moan of relief when they were finally allowed to lie down.

Despite how tired they were, they found they couldn't sleep. Every time their eyes closed, they saw Ha Beili being thrust to the ground, and every position they tried awakened some new ache. Finally, they ended up stretched out on their back as Bich's mother settled in herself, nestling her granddaughter against her side beside Chih.

The toddler whined, tugging hard at her grandmother's sleeping robe, and when her grandmother disentangled her hand, her whines increased in volume. Her grandmother sighed.

"What? What does precious little treasure want, hm?"

"Talk-story!"

"Can little treasure ask politely?"

"No."

"Can little treasure try?"

"Grandma, please. Talk-story, *please.*"

Is that all I have to do? Chih thought with amusement, and then Bich's mother began to speak.

All right, this happened a long, long time ago, back when the rocks and stones were still soft. Back then, we Pha lived on the plains, where the sky is a great white bowl that rests upon the grasslands, curved overhead to protect us from the warring of the things beyond.

Things were easier back then. Bees had no stingers so you could scoop honey straight out of the hive, and if you wanted a big peach to eat, all you had to do was to whistle and it would drop into your hands. The fish jumped out of the rivers with no need for a net, and the water bison had so much milk they would nurse tiger cubs.

Today the bees protect their honey with vicious stings, and if you whistle, all you will get is your grandmother whistling back to you. The fish stay in the rivers, the tigers nurse their own cubs, and this all happened because one day, the sun ran away.

There came a terrible rumbling in the earth and a thundering roar, as if some beast had been loosed. It was so terrifying that the sun threw her gray silk scarf over her head and jumped down from her chair in the sky, running so far and so fast she dropped straight over the edge of the earth. Oh we called for her and cried for her, but she was gone, and without her, the world grew dark and cold.

Sometimes the moon came to comfort us, but she was inconstant, always concerned with other people who might love her better, and the only things that you can grow by moonlight are bitter and mean.

We gathered around our hearths, and we kept our fires lit. It was all we could do, sit and try to stay warm as we hoped for the sun to return to us.

Among the Pha back then there was a little girl, and her name was Thi—

"Me!"

"Yes, a little girl named Thi, just like you!"

—and Thi was a very good little girl who always did what she was told, except for one thing. She loved stories, all stories. She loved the ones told by her mother and her father, the ones told by her aunts and uncles, the ones told by her grandmother the most of all. However, as she listened to her family talk into the long night, she realized something. She knew why the rabbit hid his golden horns, and why green whales sing the same songs no matter where they live. She knew of the scholar who married a tiger and the wild pig who married a corpse. She knew all the stories her people told, and she was so bored by them.

One night, she glanced out over the dark grasslands, and she saw a light flickering far across the plain. Ever since the sun had run away, there had never been such a thing. The only light came from the Pha hearths; all else was darkness. It could have been a ghost burning itself up to get warm, it could have been a one-eyed tiger, but instead Thi knew immediately that it was a fire with someone there tending it. If there was someone tending it, why, there must be someone with new stories to tell, and with a cry of joy, Thi ran towards the glow.

She ran and she ran and she ran, but no matter how far she ran, the fire never seemed to get any closer. Perhaps another girl would have given up and gone home, but no other Pha girl loved stories as much as Thi did, and so she just ran harder. When she tripped and landed in a puddle, she kicked off her shoes to keep running. When she struck her bare foot on a boulder, she wailed, but she jumped over the boulder, and kept running.

She ran and ran and ran, and finally, she came to the fire—only it was no fire at all, but the sun, hiding with her gray silk shawl over her head. She had been so frightened by the noise that she shivered with fear, and Thi, who was a very kind little girl, came to sit with her and hold her hand like her parents did with Thi when she was afraid.

She held the sun's hand, and she sang to her, and when she could not think of what else to do, she started to tell her stories. She told the sun about the rabbit who hid his golden horns and why the green whales all sing the same songs and the scholar who married a tiger and the wild pig who married a corpse. Thi told the sun all of the stories that the Pha people knew, and because the sun had never heard them before, she was not bored at all.

Soon the sun was so entertained by Thi's stories that she forgot to be afraid. When she gasped at the story of the siege of the cranes, her shawl fell off her head and light returned to the world.

Now Thi could look around, and she saw that she was in a new land, very different from her home on the plains. Here, the sky was an enormous plate held up by the mountains, and the trees were so old she couldn't ring them with her arms outstretched.

Before she could become alarmed, though, her mother and her father and her grandmother, and indeed all of the Pha, came out of the trees. They had seen her run off, and of course they came running after her. Where one of us goes, we all go, and they marveled at how far they had run chasing after Thi. The puddle she had splashed through, that was the sea, and the boulder she had leaped, that was Mount Wreckram. They were so far from where they had come from, but look, they had found their dear Thi, and they had found the sun again.

They stayed in their new home in the mountains, and they grew durian and cassava and rice to eat, and they cast nets into the Ya-lé River for fat fish heavy with red eggs. They told old stories about their old home and new stories about their new home. And as for Thi, she lived a hundred wonderful years and heard ten thousand wonderful stories, and the sun shone on her for all her days.

Chih put aside their notebook, stretching out their hand.

"Thank you for the story," they whispered.

Bich's mother nodded, baby Thi asleep in the crook of her arm, and Chih lay back down on the mattress. In the other room, Bich was saying something, her sister disagreeing. Beyond them was the beating of the rain, and beyond that was the quiet thunder of the Ya-lé River.

As they curled up on their side, it occurred to Chih that this life, or one very like it, could have been theirs if their parents hadn't given them to Singing Hills. There could be a warm house with a family they cared for who cared for them in return, good cooking smells and work that was the same every day. It could be sweet, and not easy, but perhaps easier. Then, without willing it, their fingers slid along the spine of the notebook by their head, half-full of names and generations remembered, the count of stories for Singing Hills greater by one.

Still, there would be stories, they thought, and then they were asleep.

Chapter Ten

The hailstones were all anyone could speak of for days. They had put holes in roofs, killed some livestock, knocked a handful of people unconscious. More were left with livid bruises or even broken bones—Chih was worried for their own fingers until the swelling started to go down and they got their flexibility back.

The rain hadn't let up since the hailstones struck, but it had lightened, going from the thunderous downpour to a misting drizzle that washed the world to shades of moonstone and labradorite. The river rose in its banks and as the last days of the festivals settled on a decidedly calmer pace, Chih and Almost Brilliant took many accounts of the storm, from the harbormaster, from the magistrate, from the courtesan who owned the tallest house in Luntien, from Bich and her cousin, and of course from Ha Beili.

"Dunno why you want my account," she said after she

was done. "I didn't see much from under all those angry idiots."

"It is in the interests of the clerics of Singing Hills to make their accounts as complete as it is possible to do so," said Almost Brilliant from Chih's shoulder.

"If we didn't take your account, there would be a silence where you should be," Chih said, and Ha Beili muttered something about clerics who screamed like monkeys before turning away.

They hadn't needed anyone at Certain Compassion, but Bich had asked around until she found an aunt who wanted some help at her fish stall. Ha Beili had a pallet in the aunt's front room and all the muddy fish she could eat, and she was, as she told Chih, getting used to smelling like the bottom of the river all the time. When Chih had asked tentatively about her family, her face grew hard, and she shook her head. Not now. Maybe sometime or maybe not ever, but not now.

Still, a few days after Chih took her account, she showed up at Certain Compassion at the end of Chih's shift.

"I told you about Muyi," she said diffidently. "Some of us, we're going to go say hello. You know."

It was more than some of them. It was the largest number of Muyese Chih had seen away from the temple, and in the steady drizzle, they made their way to one of the deserted pavilions along the river. The pavilions had housed the animal showings, and they would be torn down when the festival was over. They still smelled faintly of horse and pig, but they'd been strung with flower garlands, the floor swept, and a trio of musicians, two lutists and a drummer, were set up at the far end. Almost Brilliant, tired of crowds, fluttered up to the rafters, and Chih and Ha Beili lingered by the railing, the sound of the rushing river behind them almost drowning out the excited talk of the gathered Muyese. There were girls circulating through the crowd carrying trays piled high with flowers, purchased by the armful from florists departing the festival. Ha Beili took some red and white blooms, tucking one into Chih's robe, weaving herself a crown for her head.

Ha Beili stuck by Chih's side until some of her friends cried her name, grabbing her and bearing her away like a treasure they had lost. Chih watched her go, and then made their way to a sheltered spot by the musicians, asking for their names and the names of the songs they played. It was much like the community gatherings they had been to in the past, following Cleric Thien or Cleric Sun, people remembering who they were and what they cared for.

Without any signal Chih could see, a middle-aged woman took a teenage girl's hands in hers, and they started to dance. Almost immediately, the people around them joined hands in pairs as the musicians shifted to a different melody. There was no pattern to the pairings; they saw Vang Kao partnered with a man his own age, a grandmother with a young man with arms bared to show off his extravagant tattoos. It should have been chaos, and perhaps it was as people missed turns or tripped, but it came to Chih that it was breath, the inhale and exhale of a people on the move. Chih had mostly seen the Muyese crowded and crouched, afraid; this was the Muyese moving for the pleasure of it, who they had been on Muyi, who they still were, who they really were.

"They're breathing again," Chih whispered, and then they yelped as Almost Brilliant came down from the rafters to settle on their shoulder. They blushed; it was a silly thing to say when the clerics of Singing Hills were witnesses, not poets, but Almost Brilliant made a satisfied sound, preening the curve of Chih's ear.

"They are."

When the music ended, the Muyese went to the railing and cast the flowers they wore into the river below. The flowers clustered together in the water as they were carried away into the night. They floated downstream, good wishes and love carried back to the sea, maybe all the way back to a lonely god who did not know where her people had gone.

Throat tight, Chih threw the flower from their robe into the water to join the others, and then they went back to the restaurant to write it all down.

Things had slowed down enough that Chih could be spared from the restaurant in the afternoon. Their pay packet was due to catch up to them any day now, but in the meantime, they'd started working for the temple of the Lady of the Thousand Hands, setting up an inventory system that should prevent the mess in the shed from happening ever again.

Chih had rigged an awning over the storeroom door, keeping the water out but letting fresh air and light inside. This morning they'd found a series of thin-walled wooden boxes of the kind Singing Hills used to store records of official imperial edicts and rulings of the highest courts in Anh. They were, Almost Brilliant reported eagerly, the very sorts of records that had earned Singing Hills the ire of the Emperor of Nails and Storms. Singing Hills' refusal to give up their own reckonings led to decades of banishment, and Chih was almost sick from excitement when they turned over the first box. The disappointment of the broken seal and the emptiness inside was intense, but Almost Brilliant had been unexpectedly philosophical.

"Well, it is still a record," she said, and Chih saw, as she had, the characters carved inside the lid of the box they held: *given to the keeping of Cleric Lunmo of Singing Hills.* All of the boxes were the same, the responsibility of Cleric Lunmo of Singing Hills, who had come so far and told stories to their grandchildren. Her grandchildren? Chih didn't know. They wished Cleric Lunmo was still around to ask, even if she asked to be called Old Mo. They wondered if they would answer them or if she would, perhaps as she had all her life, only shake her head and never speak of where she had come from.

Still, there was a name they could bring back. It was

far from nothing, and when Chih reached for the last box to do their due diligence, they were not expecting more. This box, however, was heavier than the others, and when they opened it, they found it had been packed so tightly with wood shavings that they bounced out when the latch was drawn.

"Be careful," Almost Brilliant murmured, and Chih nodded, sitting on the floor and brushing the wood shavings aside.

Carefully, they uncovered a cloth bundle, lavender silk noil, still shiny, sewn shut. Chih hesitated, and then, glancing at Almost Brilliant who watched from the handle of an ancient iron hoe nearby, they cut the stitches open with their knife.

"Oh," they said softly, taking in the thin slivers of the beak, the high arches of bone where the eyes had rested, the claws curled up tight. The feathers were dusty, somewhat leached of color, but it was clear to see that once, they had been black, orange, and white, the same as Almost Brilliant's own.

"Cover them, oh cover them, please," Almost Brilliant cried, and hurriedly, Chih did, wrapping the hoopoe's body up in silk and sewing her shroud shut with needle and thread from their mending kit. As their needle ducked in and out of the holes that the previous sewist had made—Cleric Lunmo, for who else could it be—Chih noticed how close the stitches were, how secure they would hold the hoopoe who had come all this way with their cleric. Sovann had said that her mother was young when she came from the west. Perhaps their hoopoe companion had been old, or perhaps there had been an accident of some sort, that Sovann and her children had never known a bird that dropped stories.

Except, Chih thought, *they did, if only through the stories they had been told.*

After Chih tucked the hoopoe back into the box and turned the latch, they left the shed. They sat under the tarp as the rain came down with Almost Brilliant perched on their knee. Beyond the temple, they could hear the refugee camp stirring, people eating and fighting and laughing and crying and being people, even if they were people far from home.

"We have the names of the hoopoes who fled with the clerics and the ones who flew to the sister abbey in Tsu," said Almost Brilliant after a while. "Cleric Lunmo's name will be with my family on my father's side. They should have their hoopoe's name as well, as long as they were not hatched after the great flight. Some were."

"We may know it now," Chih said thoughtfully.

"Hm?"

"The restaurant. Certain Compassion. A wish for a kindness, a hope for the future. The name of a beloved companion, and what everyone hopes to find on a journey far from home."

"Speculation, Cleric Chih," Almost Brilliant said, regaining some of her sternness. "We do not know."

They didn't. Some days, Chih felt as if they knew absolutely nothing. Today, though, they knew that Ha Beili was getting used to smelling like fish. They knew that very soon, likely in the next four or five days, a member of the Sisterhood would show up with their pay packet and they'd leave for Beixia. They knew that sometimes, hailstones of a size to kill you were the greatest of good luck.

They knew that Cleric Lunmo, long gone and unable to answer for themself, had preserved their hoopoe companion as best they could, rather than burying them, because sometime, some way, they would both get back where they were supposed to be, to who they were supposed to be.

Chih knew that when they left Luntien, they would carry a thin-walled wooden box with them, containing the remains of a hoopoe who had died far from Singing Hills, and if they were lucky, if the gods were kind and the roads were clear, someday soon, they would get to go home.

Acknowledgments

Someday, you're going to be far from home, whether that distance is counted in miles or years. When you are, be kind to yourself, okay?

Thank you as always to my agent Diana Fox for her fantastic advice and tireless support. She's a big part of why these books exist, and I am forever grateful. Thanks also go to Stephanie Stein and Julianna Kim, who approached this project with the clear eyes, kind words, and editorial brilliance that it very much needed.

Thanks are due to everyone at Tordotcom for everything they do. Greg Collins, Christine Foltzer, Lauren Hougen, Michael Dudding, Samantha Friedlander, Jacqueline Huber-Rodriguez, Alexis Saarela, Sarah Weeks, Claire Eddy, Will Hinton, Lucille Rettino, and Devi Pillai, these books would not be what they are without you!

The gorgeous cover art for *A Long and Speaking Silence* is the work of the incredible Alyssa Winans—go check out her stuff, it's fantastic!

For my friends, new and old, I love you—thank you for loving me.

About the Author

CJ Foeckler

Nghi Vo is the bestselling author of *Siren Queen*, *The Chosen and the Beautiful*, *Don't Sleep with the Dead*, and *The City in Glass*, as well as the acclaimed novellas of the Singing Hills Cycle, which began with *The Empress of Salt and Fortune*. Her work has been nominated for the Nebula, Locus, and Lambda Literary Awards and the LA Times and Ursula K. Le Guin Prizes, and has won the Crawford, Ignyte, and Hugo Awards. Born in Illinois, she now lives on the shores of Lake Michigan. She believes in the ritual of lipstick, the power of stories, and the right to change your mind.